THE SLAVES OF LOVE

Yamina froze as a new wave of terror swept over her.

Life had become so dangerous. Caught in Constantinople during the Crimean War, the exquisite young Russian had been forced to seek refuge in a Sultan's harem from a mob that would have torn her apart. And when the harem became too perilous—not to her life but her virtue—Yamina had to flee again.

Hidden in the bottom of an Oriental trunk masquerading as a gift from the Sultan, she was carried aboard a ship in the harbor. Yamina felt she was safe at last. Until she heard the voice of the man accepting the Sultan's gift—a man she despised.

She would rather be back in the harem—or dead at the bottom of the Bosporus Straits—than be imprisoned aboard ship with such a monster!

BARBARA CARTLAND

Bantam Books by Barbara Cartland
Ask your bookseller for the books you have missed

1 THE DARING DECEPTION
2 NO DARKNESS FOR LOVE
3 THE LITTLE ADVENTURE
4 LESSONS IN LOVE
5 JOURNEY TO PARADISE
6 THE BORED BRIDEGROOM
7 THE PENNILESS PEER
8 THE DANGEROUS DANDY
9 THE RUTHLESS RAKE
10 THE WICKED MARQUIS
11 THE CASTLE OF FEAR
12 THE GLITTERING LIGHTS
13 A SWORD TO THE HEART
14 THE KARMA OF LOVE
15 THE MAGNIFICENT MARRIAGE
16 BEWITCHED
17 THE IMPETUOUS DUCHESS
18 THE FRIGHTENED BRIDE
19 THE SHADOW OF SIN
20 THE FLAME IS LOVE
21 THE TEARS OF LOVE
22 A VERY NAUGHTY ANGEL
23 CALL OF THE HEART
24 THE DEVIL IN LOVE
25 AS EAGLES FLY
26 LOVE IS INNOCENT
27 SAY YES, SAMANTHA
28 THE CRUEL COUNT
29 THE MASK OF LOVE
30 FIRE ON THE SNOW
31 AN ARROW OF LOVE
32 A GAMBLE WITH HEARTS
33 A KISS FOR THE KING
34 A FRAME OF DREAMS
35 THE FRAGRANT FLOWER
36 THE ELUSIVE EARL
37 MOON OVER EDEN
38 THE GOLDEN ILLUSION
39 THE HUSBAND HUNTERS
40 NO TIME FOR LOVE
41 PASSIONS IN THE SAND
42 THE SLAVES OF LOVE
43 AN ANGEL IN HELL

Barbara Cartland

The Slaves of Love

THE SLAVES OF LOVE

A Bantam Book/July 1976

ISBN 0-553-02802-2

Published simultaneously in the United States and Canada

Bantam Books are published by Bantam Books, Inc. Its trademark, consisting of the words "Bantam Books" and the portrayal of a bantam, is registered in the United States Patent Office and in other countries. Marca Registrada. Bantam Books, Inc., 666 Fifth Avenue, New York, New York 10019.

PRINTED IN THE UNITED STATES OF AMERICA

Author's Note

The descriptions of the Sultan's Harem are accurate. Sebastopol fell in September 1855 and the terms of peace concluded in January 1856.

King Otho of Greece was finally deposed in 1862.

Viscount Stratford de Redcliffe was one of the greatest Ambassadors Great Britain ever had, and he won himself a unique place in diplomatic history. No other foreigner has ever dominated as he did the Turkish Empire.

The Poet Laureate Lord Tennyson wrote on his death in 1884:

Thou third great Canning, stand among our best
  And noblest, now thy long day's work has ceased,
Here silent is our Minister of the West
  Who wert the voice of England in the East.

Chapter 1

1855

Lord Castleford, galloping over the uneven ground which was bright with wild grasses and flowers brilliant against the darkness of cypress trees, was conscious of a feeling of well-being.

After travelling for many weeks and being immersed in diplomatic meetings and memoranda, it was a joy to feel free and for the moment away from it all.

It was a brilliant Summer's day, the air was clear as crystal, and reining in his horse he looked down at the City to which in the past all the civilised world had brought learning, art, riches, and splendour.

Some of the glory of Constantinople had faded, but from the distance the glitter of the domes and spires, the vistas of marble colonnades, the great Palaces with their parapets and gilded balconies laden with sculpture still stirred the imagination.

It was several years since Lord Castleford had been in Turkey, and he thought as he looked on its sun-kissed Capital that the real beauty of Constantinople lay in its water.

From where he stood there was water everywhere, clear, blue, shimmering away into the placid Sea of Marmora.

To the North there was the narrow Strait of the Bosporus teeming with barges, caiques, launches, boats, and the battleships of Britain, France, and Turkey, carrying troops to the Crimea.

Below him lay the glittering loveliness of the Golden Horn which bisected the densest portion of the City, lending a strange and marvellous grace to all it touched.

As he thought of the town below him Lord Castleford remembered that he had not yet, as he had intended, purchased a present for his host, the British Ambassador, the recently ennobled Lord Stratford de Redcliffe.

He had intended to bring him a gift from Persia, where he had been a special delegate to the Shah.

But he had in fact had little time when he was in Teheran, and what he had been offered seemed too ordinary and commonplace to be a fitting present for the venerated, autocratic, and universally admired "Great Elchi," who had reformed the Ottoman Empire.

Caftans, however well embroidered, jewelled sword-hilts, or gold brocades he already had in profusion, and Lord Castleford sought something unique for the man whom he admired most amongst all others and who he frequently said had taught him all he knew of diplomacy.

On an impulse he decided to seek now, while he was out alone, some treasure hidden away in the shops of gold- and silver-work which the many ardent collectors who frequented Constantinople had not yet discovered.

He remembered one particular place where on a previous visit he had found mementos of the past when Greeks and Romans had left their imprint on what was now Turkey.

Many of their treasures had been secreted away or hidden in tombs until some thief or excavator had brought them into the light of day.

"There must be something which Lord Stratford would really appreciate," Lord Castleford murmured to himself.

As he turned his horse away from the open country towards the loveliest Capital in the world, he could see many of its great monuments.

The vast oblong of the Hippodrome with its four rows of pavilions and galleries; the huge Basilica of Santa Sophia, drawing the eye of the faithful at all moments of the day.

Besides these, there was a profusion of glittering minarets and domes, all stirring the imagination, recorded in history, sung in verse, envied through the centuries by less-opulent peoples.

Below him Lord Castleford could see the Top Kapou Serai, or the Seraglio, which only the previous year had been forsaken by the Sultan for the Dolmabahce Palace.

The cypress trees massed round it gave it a strangely evil appearance.

A place redolent of love, murder, beauty, ambition, and torture through the ages, of dark deeds and fretted fountains, of gilded kiosks and hideous deaf mutes.

Of unwanted women and dispensable Sultans being cast from its walls into the silent bosom of the Bosporus.

There death walked with life, beauty with decay, crude naked crime with the softness of young virgins, evil with the songs of birds.

The Seraglio, once the heart of the City!

Lord Castleford soon found himself riding in the Bazaar where Justinian had once stabled two thousand horses but where now there were open shops selling every kind of embroidery, gold-work, armour, cloth, provisions, all mingled with the colourful vegetables and fruit for which the Bosporus was famous.

In the narrow twisting alley-ways of the Bazaar the people in themselves were a kaleidoscope of colour.

There were Armenians with coloured sashes, glaring out of rags and bearing heavy loads, veiled women with long mantles and yashmaks, blind beggars in threadbare turbans stretching out bony hands for *bakshish,* fat Pashas under sun-shades held by attendants, Persians dyed by the Eastern sun in their sheepskin caps and fur pelisses.

Donkeys and lean horses staggered almost invisible under every sort of load.

It was all part of the East that Lord Castleford knew and loved.

His eyes did not miss an old Turk with a tray of sweet-meats on his head, Dervishes in white turbans and long, dark caftans, and Turkish Officers in their red fezes trotting by on their well-bred horses.

He moved on, taking no notice of those who solicited him as he passed and tried to tempt him with bales of Eastern wool, Bulgarian embroidered satins, Persian carpets woven wholly in silk, delicate silks from Brussa in every hue and texture.

He was just beginning to think he must have lost his way and forgotten where the shop he sought was situated, when suddenly there was a noise and confusion ahead.

The cry of shrill voices gradually became a roar of crying, hooting, and shrieking.

Those round Lord Castleford looked apprehensively in the direction from which the noise was coming and even the most lethargic were suddenly alert.

A number of men came running down the narrow

thoroughfare, many of them carrying sticks and apparently dragging with them someone or something which was for the moment indistinguishable.

Hastily Lord Castleford moved his horse as near as possible to an adjacent wall, and the street-sellers pulled as many of their goods as they could within the confines of their tiny cavern-like shops.

But already vegetables were being upset, fruit rolled on the ground, and the noise made by the invaders was magnified by the protestations and recriminations of those whose wares were damaged.

Lord Castleford's horse pricked his ears and fidgeted a little, but he was too well trained to be frightened by the din or even the sticks of those advancing upon them.

His Lordship edged him forward a little to where the street seemed wider. Then he saw that standing immediately at his side there was a European woman in a white gown.

Obviously frightened, she was standing with her back against the side of the shop. She had climbed onto a narrow step to be out of the way. Standing in front of her was a Turk who was clearly her servant.

Lord Castleford was well aware that no lady would go shopping without having a servant in attendance and even so, few women ventured into the Bazaar.

She was very quietly dressed and, although her skirts were full, she was not wearing a fashionable crinoline. But she had, he could see, a very elegant figure, small, slim, and was obviously very young.

As the crowds reached them, surging round, shrieking, and yelling, the noise was deafening, and now Lord Castleford could hear what they were saying:

"Kill him!" "Destroy him!" "Torture him!" "An informer—a spy—he must die!"

It was then that he could see in the centre of the crowd a man being dragged along by his arms, his legs, his clothing, and his hair. His face running with blood, his eyes half-closed.

It was obvious that he was more dead than alive and Lord Castleford guessed that he was, or so the crowd believed, a Russian spy.

War always engenders witch-hunts and easily inflames a mob.

His Lordship had already learnt on his arrival at Constantinople that the City was in the grip of "spy fever" and that the Turks were ready to suspect of being Russian any stranger who could not account for his nationality.

The man the crowd had captured was being beaten with sticks by those who were not carrying him, kicked and spat upon, and subjected all the time to an unintelligible but nevertheless very violent form of abuse.

As the rioters came level with Lord Castleford they slowed their progress, owing to the men in front of them being blocked where the road narrowed.

Seated on his horse, Lord Castleford could see that the victim who had incurred the wrath of the mob looked, beneath his wounds, to be a man of some culture and of a better class than those who were persecuting him.

"Is there . . . nothing we can . . . do?"

For a moment he wondered who had spoken. Then he saw that the lady who was pressed against the wall beside him was bending towards him so as to make herself heard.

She spoke in English although he realised she had a foreign accent.

"Unfortunately nothing can be done," he replied almost sharply. "To get embroiled with this mob, considering we are also foreigners, would be to court disaster."

"But he may have done nothing . . . wrong."

"They believe him to be a spy—a Russian!"

"That is what I thought," the lady said, "but they may be mistaken."

"Perhaps they are," Lord Castleford replied, "but it is not for us to interfere. In fact, quite frankly, we simply dare not do so."

Even as he spoke, the crowd, still shouting and screaming, moved on, brushing against his horse and causing the animal to fidget.

The man who had been hit and knocked about all the time they had paused now seemed to be unconscious as they carried him with them.

There were still stragglers coming down the narrow street, and it was obvious that several of the younger men working in the shops, or perhaps the proprietors' sons, were ready to join in and see the fun.

"We should get away from here as quickly as possible!" Lord Castleford said.

He knew only too well that mob violence was something which could spread and intensify rapidly, and that one fight usually led to another. The Bazaar would not be a safe place to be in until everything had quieted down again.

He looked at the woman standing beside him.

"If you would ride in front of me on my saddle," he said, "I think it would be safer for you than attempting to walk."

As he spoke he glanced at the road ahead and saw, as he had suspected, that many more men were hurrying to join the throng which had just passed them. The woman must have seen it too, because she said quickly:

"That would be very kind."

She turned to her servant, who was still standing in front of her, and Lord Castleford saw that he was a middle-aged Turk with a quiet, respectable appearance.

"Go home, Hamid," the lady said. "This gentleman will take care of me. I do not think it wise for me to walk any further."

"That is true, Mistress."

Lord Castleford bent towards her, she put up her arms, and he lifted her onto the saddle in front of him.

She was so light that she seemed almost to fly into the position he intended, sitting sideways so that with his left arm he could hold her in place while he held the reins with his right.

The bonnet she wore tied under her chin was a small one and did not impede her from leaning back against him, making it easy for him to control his horse without her being in any way an encumbrance.

Slowly, without haste, Lord Castleford edged his mount forward with an expert hand, keeping as close as possible to the walls and drawing frequently to a standstill to allow the crowds to pass.

Fortunately everyone was so intent on joining the rioters ahead of them, whose shouts could still be heard, that they did not trouble themselves with either Lord Castleford or his burden.

After a short distance he turned into a narrow alley to the left which held nothing more fearsome than a few tired-looking donkeys bringing fresh provisions into the City from the villages outside.

Soon they were clear even of the alley-ways, and after passing a Mosque and a few unimportant houses they were on open ground.

"I think we would be wise at the moment to make a detour," Lord Castleford said. "If you will tell me where you live we will approach the City from the other side, which will certainly be safer and more savoury than the way I have just come."

He had an idea where the crowd was taking its prisoner, but he intended to take no chances.

At the rumour of an execution, with or without the law, mobs would be hastening from all parts of the City, and although they had been fortunate so far in escaping without incident, the execution of one foreigner might easily make the crowds thirst for the execution of others.

"That poor man!" the lady Lord Castleford was conveying said in a soft voice. "I cannot bear to . . . think of what he is . . . suffering!"

"I imagine he is past having feelings of any sort by now," Lord Castleford replied.

Now that they were safe, he looked at her for the first time and realised she was in fact very lovely.

She looked different, he thought, from any woman he had seen before and he wondered what nationality she was.

She was certainly not English, although she spoke the language extremely well. Her eyes were very large and dark and her hair was dark too.

But her skin, which had an almost magnolia quality about it, was very white.

Looking down at her, he could see that her face was heart-shaped with a small pointed chin. She had a tiny, straight nose and her mouth, he thought, was almost perfect in its soft curves.

It struck him immediately that she was far too beautiful to be walking about Constantinople with only the protection of one elderly Turkish servant.

Because he was curious he asked:

"I think we should introduce ourselves. I am English and my name is Castleford—Lord Castleford. I am staying at the British Embassy."

"I am French, *Monsieur*, and I am extremely grateful to you for coming to my rescue."

She spoke in French, a correct, classical French that was quite faultless, and yet Lord Castleford thought she did not actually look or even sound French.

Then he told himself that living away from her own country she might easily be harder to identify than if he had in fact met her in France.

"And your name?" he enquired.

"Yamina."

He raised his eye-brows.

"That is hardly a French name."

"I have lived in this part of the world all my life."

That accounted for the fact that she did not seem French, he thought.

He realised too that she did not wish to give him her surname and, although he wished that she would assuage his curiosity, at the same time he applauded her prudence.

After all, they had met only casually, and a well-bred young woman would not be precipitate in becoming closely acquainted with a stranger.

"Will you tell me where you live?" he asked.

She explained and he looked a trifle surprised.

It was near one of the outer walls of the City and he knew there were few houses in that vicinity in which a European would live.

Because he was definitely intrigued by the woman sitting elegantly in front of him, he did not hurry his horse but walked him quietly over the grass-covered ground.

"You like Constantinople?" he asked conversationally.

"Sometimes I hate it!" she answered. "As I did a few minutes ago, when the crowd was being so cruel, even bestial!"

There was a little tremor in her voice and Lord Castleford knew she was still unhappy over the spy who had doubtless suffered torture and, even if he were now dead, was still being abused.

"The Turk can be very cruel," he said. "At the same time, he is a good fighter and is, I hear, highly commended by the British and the French for his fighting qualities in the Crimea."

"It is a senseless, unnecessary War!" Yamina replied.

"I agree with you, and Heaven knows our Ambassador did everything he could to prevent it."

"Not very successfully!" Yamina answered, and there was a touch of sarcasm in her voice.

"The Russians were impossible!" Lord Castleford exclaimed. "After all, it was they who bombarded Sinope on the South coast of the Black Sea, destroying a Turkish Squadron."

"Perhaps they had reason," Yamina suggested.

"Reason?" Lord Castleford ejaculated sharply. "The conflict at Sinope was more like a slaughter than a battle, rather what you have just seen in the Bazaar on a smaller scale."

Yamina did not speak and after a moment he went on:

"The excellent behaviour of the Turkish land-forces aroused the sympathy and admiration of Europe. You cannot be surprised that last year Great Britain and France declared war on Russia."

"All war is wrong and wicked!" Yamina said violently.

Lord Castleford smiled.

"That is a woman's point of view. Sometimes war means justice, and that is what we are seeking in our support of the Turks."

"I only hope that the men on both sides who are being killed in the effort appreciate what you are doing for them," Yamina remarked.

Now there was no doubt that she was being sarcastic.

"You do not sound as if you are whole-heartedly in support of your countrymen and mine in this War, which, I would remind you, started originally from a dispute over the guardianship of the Holy Places in Jerusalem."

"That question was settled two years ago," Yamina said sharply.

Lord Castleford was surprised that she was so knowledgeable.

There was a faint smile on his lips as he said:

"I agree the question was settled by the British, Russian, and French Ambassadors. But then, as doubtless you know, the Russian Ambassador, Menshikov, demanded further Russian rights which could not be acceded to by the Turks."

Lord Castleford's voice was cold as he went on:

"He was very aggressive and, in my opinion, he was determined to force Turkey into a humiliating position."

"Do you really think that . . . we can win this War?" Yamina asked in a low voice, and there was just a little pause before the word "we" which Lord Castleford noticed.

"I am certain we can!" he replied. "Our troops have suffered acutely during the Winter months in the

Crimea, but now at last we are becoming more organised, and I do not think it will be long before the Tsar asks for our peace terms."

Yamina was silent and they rode on.

The sunshine was warm on their faces and the scent of the flowers mingled with the soft salt breeze blowing in from the sea.

She was very light against Lord Castleford's arms and he knew this was due entirely to her poise and grace, which made her sit on a saddle without a pummel as if it was no effort at all.

"Do you often ride yourself?" he asked, following the trend of his thoughts.

"I used to," she replied, "but not lately. It is a pleasure being on a horse such as this."

"It belongs to the Ambassador," Lord Castleford explained, "and he is as good a judge of horse-flesh as he is about everything else."

"You admire him?"

"Who does not admire him when he is more important even than the Sultan? It was said often enough in the past that Sir Stratford Canning was the real King of Turkey, and now that he is back again, it is still true."

There was an enthusiasm in Lord Castleford's voice that had not been there previously.

Yamina glanced up at him.

She had thought at first that, although he was handsome, he seemed cold and austere with that superior English attitude which, in common with most other people, she found disconcerting.

For the moment the warmth in his voice surprised her, even while she told herself that she was sure he was far too busy admiring himself to admire anyone else.

He was not the type of man whom she thought attractive, though at the same time she knew that she must be grateful to him for rescuing her from what might have been a very difficult, if not dangerous, situation.

It was taking them some time to reach the District where she lived, but she was well aware that Lord Castleford had been wise in avoiding streets in which they might have encountered more violence.

Now they were descending between the dark cypresses and bushes covered with white and yellow blossoms.

"You must be more careful another time," Lord Castleford said, almost as if he spoke to a child, "before you go shopping with only one elderly servant to protect you."

"It is something I do not often do," Yamina replied. "But my father is ill and I needed some special herbs. I wished to discuss with the herbist what would be most suitable."

"Would it not have been wiser to call in a Physician?" Lord Castleford asked.

"In this part of the world there are herbal remedies for almost every ailment," Yamina answered. "Many of them have been handed down for centuries by word of mouth, from family to family, from father to son. They are not written down, they do not appear in books, but nevertheless they are extremely efficacious."

"But surely taking them without guidance is somewhat of a risk?" Lord Castleford persisted.

"No more of a risk than accepting blindly what is ordered by a Physician," Yamina replied.

She paused, and then as if she could not help taunting him she said:

"From what we have heard of the Hospital arrangements at Scutari, the Physicians have produced little or nothing to help the men who have been wounded in the War."

"There you are right!" Lord Castleford agreed. "But I assure you it is most unjust and unfair to blame Lord Stratford, as the Press in England has been doing."

"So the British are incensed!" Yamina exclaimed. "I am glad about that!"

"The administrative muddle, I am perfectly prepared to admit, has been a disgrace!" Lord Castleford said scathingly. "At the same time, our Ambassador here was kept in ignorance through sheer departmental jealousy!"

He paused to add more quietly:

"But the Ambassadress, Lady Stratford, has certainly tried to right a wrong and now everything possible is being done to help Miss Florence Nightingale."

Yamina did not answer and after a moment he said:

"You have heard of Miss Nightingale?"

"Everyone, I think, has heard of her," Yamina replied. "The Turkish newspapers are full of stories of her courage, even though naturally the people here still believe that a woman should be veiled. They are horrified at the idea of female Nurses!"

"And you?" Lord Castleford asked. "You do not feel like joining Miss Nightingale in her campaign, not only to bring relief to our suffering soldiers but also to establish once and for all that women have a place, even in war?"

There was a slightly taunting note in his voice, as if, just as Yamina had tried to score off him, he would score off her.

"As it happens, I am at the moment in the position of being a Nurse," she answered after a moment. "My father is very ill."

"I am sorry about that," Lord Castleford said.

"And because I know how necessary I am to him," Yamina went on, "I think that women should be Nurses whether a nation is at war or peace."

"There I must disagree with you," he replied. "In the past we have always managed to fight wars without women being involved, and quite frankly I am absolutely convinced they are more of a nuisance than a help."

Yamina smiled and it seemed to illuminate her small face.

"That is just what I would expect you to say, My Lord," she remarked, and there was a note of satisfaction in her voice.

"Meaning that I am bigoted and old-fashioned?" Lord Castleford enquired.

"You put the words into my mouth," she answered sweetly, and he had a feeling they had declared war against each other.

It could not but amuse him.

She was so small and so lovely, and he thought there was something mysterious and in a way very Eastern about her.

Perhaps it was the mystery in her dark eyes. Perhaps it was her faint fragrance which he found hard to identify. It might have been the scent of jasmine or tuberose, or perhaps a mixture of them both.

He only knew it was different from any scent he had ever known before, and it had a strange allure that he could not describe even to himself. He was also aware that her body was very soft and not straight-backed as most women were.

"Will Your Lordship stop here?" Yamina asked unexpectedly.

He drew his horse to a standstill and saw just ahead there was an opening in the City Wall and through it a long flight of steps, steps that must have been built many years ago, perhaps by the Romans.

The marble was cracked and broken in places but was still usable.

"If I go this way," Yamina explained, following the direction of his eyes, "I can reach my house far quicker than by road."

As she spoke she slipped from the saddle to the ground and stood to look up at him, her eyes on his.

"I am grateful!" she said quietly.

Lord Castleford also dismounted, and now holding his horse by the bridle he put out his hand, saying:

"I am glad to have been of assistance. May I perhaps call tomorrow and see that you are no worse for the adventure?"

Yamina shook her head.

"I am afraid my father is too ill for us to receive any guests at the moment."

"Then may I perhaps leave a card asking for news of his health?" Lord Castleford persisted.

She gave him a smile which told him that she was amused by his insistence. At the same time, she had no intention of giving way to his inquisitiveness.

"I can only repeat what I have already said, My Lord," she said. "Good-bye! I have been most interested in our conversation."

She turned away as she spoke, without taking the hand he stretched out to her.

She descended the steps, and he could only stand looking somewhat helpless as she moved with a grace that kept him watching her until finally she disappeared out of sight.

She did not turn round, she did not wave, she just walked out of his life. And he found it extremely irritating to realise that he knew no more about her than when they had first met.

Yamina was her name, but Yamina who?

She was cultured, she was a lady, but why need she be so secretive?

There was no doubt, Lord Castleford thought as he rode back to the Embassy, that she was well informed.

It surprised him that she should know so much about the War, and he could not help agreeing with her that it was a confrontation which should have been avoided. Yet, from a diplomatic point of view, it was difficult to see how.

The Russians had been deliberately aggressive, determined not to accept the peace terms which Lord Stratford had tried so hard to persuade everyone to accept.

As for the scandal of the Hospital at Scutari and the lack of necessary medical supplies, this was the fault of the medical authorities themselves.

They had deliberately kept the British Ambassador in the dark as to their needs. But an appeal to the Foreign Office for aid that should have been furnished by the War Office was in their eyes a worse crime than letting their patients die.

When the Ambassador learnt the truth and realised what was happening in the Hospital, he did all he could to provide for the wounded.

More Houses were turned into Hospitals, including one of the Sultan's Palaces, and the Turks were forced to provide a Steamer to carry provisions every day across the Bosporus.

Finally Lord Stratford had even demanded accommodation for the sick and wounded Russians, a human touch with which not everyone was in agreement.

It was his insistence which had changed the whole medical situation since last year, although Lord Castleford was aware it would be a long time before people forgot the horrors, the privations, and the unnecessary deaths that occurred in the first months of the War.

But what he did not expect was to find a Frenchwoman looking like Yamina, who had almost challenged him on the subject and had forced him into defending the position of the British Ambassador.

He was used to the English in Constantinople fawning like the Turks on Lord Stratford, speaking about him as if he were an angel sent from Heaven to stand at the door of the East with a flaming sword, maintaining order for the rest of Europe.

Alternatively, he would listen to the scarcely veiled jealousy of the French.

Their Ambassador was not so effective, and they were always complaining that they were being slighted or not kept completely in the picture as regards the conduct of the War itself.

This was not surprising. Lord Stratford had said to Lord Castleford the night before:

"Great Britain and France are a difficult pair to drive together in harness, for France regards it as a tandem in which she is the leader!"

"Surely Sebastopol should fall soon?" Lord Castleford replied. "And then perhaps honour will be satisfied as far as France is concerned."

Lord Stratford smiled a little wryly.

"Success in the field is what Napoloen III needs as a halo of glory to hide the tawdriness of his diadem!"

He sighed before he continued:

"The French want the battle to be theirs, and they do everything they possibly can to hamper the Turkish troops from achieving a victory before they can claim one for themselves."

"What a mess!" Lord Castleford exclaimed.

"Is war ever anything else?" Lord Stratford asked bitterly.

Entering the British Embassy, Lord Castleford had heard that his host was alone and joined him in one of the magnificent rooms overlooking a garden filled with flowers and in which a fountain was playing.

"Have you enjoyed your ride, Vernon?" the Ambassador asked, looking up as he entered.

Lord Stratford, at sixty-eight, was one of the most handsome men Lord Castleford had ever seen.

His hair was already white, but his earnest, astute, grey eyes seemed to penetrate into a man's inner thoughts, and a broad, massive, overhanging brow gave him an air of profound wisdom and sagacity.

It was this wisdom which had earned him the title of the "Great Elchi" and by which he was known throughout the Levant.

But the Christians who lived in the Turkish Empire used a much higher title. They called him "the Padishah of the Padishah"—the "Sultan of the Sultan."

But because of Lord Stratford's influence and authority, people of all races and religions looked to the British Embassy for protection—Nestorians, Yezidis, Naionites, Druses, dwellers in Mesopotamia, Jews and proselytes, Cretes and Arabs, all, turned for succour to the far-reaching arm of the British Ambassador.

Lord Stratford was very formidable-looking, but this was not because of his personal pride.

He was in fact an unassuming, simple, and courtly gentleman of scholarly and artistic tastes.

He enjoyed writing poetry, which he often insisted on reading aloud to his Attaches after they had been up all night copying despatches and could scarcely keep their eyes open.

He had a great sense of humour, but officially, as the Queen's representative, he considered that it was incumbent upon him to uphold the dignity and prestige of his country in his own person.

He had however a violent temper and his outbursts of rage were frightening.

The Turks quaked in their slippers if they heard he had arrived to interview one of them. But the most charming thing about Lord Stratford was that if he was in the wrong, he would make apologies and amends for words that had passed his lips in the fury of the moment.

His servants remained in his service for years, and his apologies often turned the very men he had offended into his firmest friends.

To those he called his "pupils" he taught the art of diplomacy. By them he was not only revered but loved, and Lord Castleford was one of them.

He knew how hard Lord Stratford worked, how close to his heart the Turkish nation was, and how only he could have supported, guided, and led the weak Sultan Abdul Mejia and kept him in a position of power.

Sultans had very short lives and most of them died after a very few years of reigning over little but the Harem.

Abdul Mejia not only had survived but, thanks entirely to Lord Stratford, he was respected all over the East.

"Any news from the front?" Lord Castleford asked.

"Little that is cheerful," Lord Stratford replied.

"There is trouble in the City," Lord Castleford

said. "The mob had got hold of a man they suspected of being a spy. They were dragging him through the Bazaar to execute him, although I think by the time they had reached the Square he was dead!"

Lord Stratford sighed.

"I imagined that this would gather momentum."

"The hunt for spies?"

"It happens always when there is a war, and while Sebastopol is still holding out, people in Constantinople wish to fight things their own way."

"That is understandable," Lord Castleford said. "At the same time, it could be dangerous!"

"I am aware of that," Lord Stratford said sharply. "There are people of all nationalities living in Constantinople. If some of them are Russians, they have in fact been here for years and would be incapable of spying or of being of any harm to the community. But a mob will never listen to reason."

"That is true," Lord Castleford said, thinking of the man he had seen being beaten and spat upon, and wondering if he had done anything that was wrong except by accident of birth.

"There were two or three upsets last week," Lord Stratford said, "and I believe the authorities are talking of having a systematic, official search from house to house. It is better that an investigation should be official than that the people should take the law into their own hands."

"I am sure you are right there," Lord Castleford said.

He wondered as he spoke if Yamina would be haunted by what she had seen and knew it would be difficult for him to forget the blood-stained face, the eyes closed in pain, the man's body being virtually torn to pieces by the crowd as they dragged him with them.

It was a sight that no woman should have seen, and he wished he had impressed upon her even more strongly the fact that it would be best for her not to go into the Bazaar again but stay quietly at home until the trouble was over.

He could understand her anxiety to obtain the right medicine for her father. It was not an easy task. Conventional drugs were difficult to buy and were extremely expensive.

She had been purchasing the herbs in which the countryfolk had great faith. This was not peculiar to Turkey but was true of all Asiatic and Eastern countries.

At the same time, were they effective? He was doubtful about that and he shrugged his shoulders metaphorically as he thought about them.

* * *

As it happened, Yamina was at that very moment cooking the herbs that she had found waiting for her at home.

Her servant, having returned far quicker than she had been able to do, had brought them with him.

"Now what exactly did the herbist say, Hamid?" she enquired.

She spoke Turkish quite well, but not well enough to be able to differentiate the dialects which were sometimes a mixture of Greek as well as other languages. They were often quite unintelligible to those who had not actually been born Turkish.

Hamid explained and she started to work to clean the roots meticulously before she cut them into small pieces.

"The gentleman brought you home safely, Mistress?" Hamid asked.

"As you see, quite safely!" Yamina smiled.

"A fine-looking man!" Hamid remarked. "Like the Great Elchi himself!"

"I have never seen the Elchi," Yamina replied.

"Great man, much power! Even Sultan do as he say."

"So I have heard," Yamina said dryly.

She thought it was typical of the English to get themselves into such a position of power that no-one could move without their approval.

She could imagine Lord Castleford being just as autocratic, and she told herself that she would never have anything in common with men who looked like ramrods, and who used their power as a battering-ram to get everything they wanted.

"They are not human!" she told herself.

Putting the herbs into a sauce-pan on the fire, she said to Hamid:

"I will go upstairs and see how my father is. You say he was asleep when you came back?"

"Sleeping very peacefully, Mistress. I leave him. Sleep is better than any other medicine."

"That is true," Yamina said, "and the Master has been sleeping badly lately, as you know. If the herbs do not bring down his fever, Hamid, I cannot think what we shall do."

"I will try to find Doctor, Mistress."

"No, no!" Yamina said quickly. "It would be too dangerous. We have managed all these months. It would be crazy to send for one now."

She moved towards the door as she spoke, then she realised that Hamid was looking uneasy, as if he had something to say but did not know how to say it.

She knew him so well that she could read his feelings without his having to express them and now she asked quickly:

"What is it, Hamid?"

"Bad news, Mistress!"

"Bad news?"

Yamina's voice was sharp.

"I learn in town today that they intend to search the houses—all the houses!"

"What for?" Yamina asked, even though she knew the answer.

"For Russians, Mistress!"

Yamina drew in a deep breath.

In front of her eyes she could see the spy who had

been dragged along the roadway being hit and reviled, his face pouring with blood, his eyes closing in the agony of death.

"What shall we do, Mistress?"

Hamid's question was hardly above a whisper.

"I do not know," Yamina answered. "What can we do when the Master is so ill that we dare not move him?"

She looked at the servant as she spoke, her eyes very dark and frightened in her pale face.

"We must put our trust in Allah," Hamid said, the words coming automatically to his lips.

"Allah?" Yamina cried. "I think that both Allah and my God has forsaken us."

Chapter 2

Feeling ashamed of her lack of self-control, Yamina picked up a jug of fresh lime-juice that she had made earlier in the day and put it on a tray with a glass ready to take up to her father.

The fever had made him very thirsty in the night and she knew that when he awoke he must have something cooling to drink.

As she busied herself she was aware that Hamid was watching her, and she said quietly:

"You know how grateful we are to you, Hamid. If it had not been for you, we would now be either dead or prisoners of the enemy."

Hamid did not reply and after a moment she went on:

"We have been in worse situations than this. When I have attended to the Master, you and I must try to think what we can do and . . . where we can . . . go."

Even as she spoke there was a little tremor in her voice.

She was afraid and, however much she tried to suppress it, the fear was like an animal gnawing inside her.

It had been there for a long time and was accentuated by what she had seen today: the dying man being dragged through the Bazaar, the blood on his face, the shouts, screams, and blows of those who reviled him.

It was true that they had so far been saved entirely by Hamid.

If he had not taken them away before the little town and garrison of Balaclava surrendered, it was frightening to think what might have occurred.

It now seemed to Yamina, nearly seven months later, almost impossible that she had been so blind to danger that once the Crimean War had started she and their whole household had not immediately returned to St. Petersburg.

The house in Crimea was their Summer home and somehow they imagined they would be safe even when there were rumours of troops landing in Calamita Bay, some forty miles North of Sebastopol.

But their house in the Crimea had always seemed a refuge, a place of security and peace.

It was hard to adjust themselves to any other outlook when the sun was shining, the gardens were more beautiful than Yamina could ever remember them, and her father seemed a little better than he had been the previous Winter.

The prosperity and popularity of Crimea had begun twenty-five years earlier, when the country North of the Black Sea became new Russian territory.

It was entirely due to Prince Michael Voronzov, who, having been appointed Governor of New Russia and Bessarabia, had set himself up in magnificent state at Odessa.

The Prince's brilliant administrative powers were

first demonstrated by his creation of a Paradise from what had been a wilderness.

At Odessa he encouraged commerce, built harbours, Hospitals, Colleges, an Opera House, made streets, and gathered round him an intelligent, charming, aristocratic circle of men appointed to administer the Province.

He gradually repopulated the desolate steppes, and when he introduced steam navigation to the Black Sea and arranged the import of English cattle, he also invited a number of French vini-culturists to stock and supervise the new Crimean vineyards.

Prince Voronzov was so popular and his achievements were so loudly acclaimed in Court circles that a large number of the Russian aristocracy immediately acquired Estates and started to build huge Mansions along the coast.

Yamina's father had chosen a site near the beautiful and attractive Harbour of Balaclava.

Here in the warm semi-tropical climate they planned an English flower-garden and an extensive botanical garden where the rarest of plants flourished and added, as in the Voronzov gardens, the dark mysterious cypress trees.

These trees all over the Province had an interesting history; for the first two had been planted by the Empress Catherine and Potemkin on their journey to her Southern domain.

From these two trees were grafted off the many cypress groves and alleys which were becoming a characteristic mark of the Crimean landscape.

Yamina's father spent a great deal of money on what he decided would be his permanent Summer home, but he could not rival the fantastic, extravagant luxury displayed by Prince Voronzov.

At Aloupkha, on a site rising one hundred and fifty feet sheer above the Black Sea, the Prince had built with the help of an Englishman, Edward Blore, a Palace which critics said resembled the stronghold of the Black Douglas or the Palace of the Great Mogul.

He used a special greenish stone that was quarried in the Urals and cost vast sums to transport.

Lesser mortals had to be content with marble, but nevertheless Yamina had loved her home and would not have had it any different.

As a child she could remember crying when the Summer was over and they had to return to the chilly splendour of St. Petersburg.

There she used to count the days until, as the snows melted, she knew they would soon be travelling South, back to their own special Paradise on the shores of the Black Sea.

Because her father was so ill and in any case communications were difficult, she had not realised the danger of the situation even when General Paskievich was laying siege to the Turkish fortress of Silistra with extraordinary vigour in the middle of May.

When she arrived in Constantinople, Yamina had learnt that with only Ottoman Commanders the garrison might have surrendered, but it happened that two young English Officers, Butler and Nasmyth, had thrown themselves into the beleaguered City and inspired the defenders with such zeal that the Tsar's Army was driven off.

This did not make her feel any more kindly towards the British when with France and Turkey, in what they called "an attempt to draw the eye-tooth of the Bear," they made a sudden descent on the Crimea.

"Long before then," Yamina later told herself, "we should have left!"

It would have been easy to do so. Carriages could have carried them to the nearest railway-station and, although the journey would have been difficult owing to her father's illness, he undoubtedly would have survived, as he had survived so much else.

At the time, however, he had seemed too ill to

move and she had not anticipated, nor had anyone else, that the War would escalate so quickly.

On August 30, 1854, four or five hundred vessels in which the three Armies were embarked had steamed from Varna Bay towards Sebastopol.

Even when some sixty-four thousand men were put ashore on the Crimea, life in the fortress went on as before. The stage-coaches still rattled into the town; the Russians watched the invaders, confident that they were inviolable.

On September 20, the fashionable society from Sebastopol were seated on Telegraph Hill on tiers of seats arranged as if for a race meeting.

Equipped with hampers, opera-glasses, and sunshades, they were waiting to applaud the annihilation of the British Regiments under Lord Raglan's command, who, with the French and Turks on their right, were trying to force the passage of the River Alma.

The battle was fierce and bloody, with terrible casualties on both sides, until the Russians "bolted with all haste."

The following day the little town and garrison of Balaclava found that an enormous number of allied troops were encircling them by land and war-ships were closing in from the sea.

On the hills above Balaclava the allies had begun to set up the tents and marquees of their huge encampment, and through this Port the invading British and Turkish forces of fifty thousand men had to be supplied.

On either side of the harbour-basin the ships were being moored with their sterns to the shore, leaving a central strip of water between the two rows so narrow that although a ship might sail down it, it was quite impossible to turn the vessel round.

It was only too late that the Commanders discovered that the water was so deep that the ships could scarcely find holding-ground for their anchors even close to the shore, and when there was an inshore wind they were in danger of being driven up onto the rocks.

But on that September day the sea was peaceful and Balaclava seemed a pleasant place to be.

No-one, least of all the inhabitants of the Crimea itself, guessed that the siege of Sebastopol would continue long after the first snows had arrived at the end of October and until the end of the following year.

It had been Hamid who first realised the danger when the advancing troops began to appear.

With two other faithful servants he placed Yamina's father on a stretcher and carried him away from the house just before it was taken over by the Military to become the headquarters of a Senior British Officer.

Creeping through the gardens, with Yamina walking beside her father, they hid in a fisherman's hut.

Hamid had left them and gone to find out if there was any chance of escape for them, while Yamina felt despairingly that it was only a question of time before they were discovered and taken prisoner.

Afterwards it was hard to remember in what sequence things had happened: it had all been so quick, and there had been no time to think, only to act.

By some miraculous manoeuvres of his own, Hamid had got them on board a troop-ship that was carrying back to Constantinople wounded men of the invading forces.

In the confusion and darkness, those who were in charge of the ship did not realise that as well as the wounded English, French, and Turks on board they also carried two Russians.

Fortunately Yamina could speak both English and French perfectly, and Hamid was Turkish.

He was one of the many Turks who had left Constantinople to seek lucrative employment with the rich Russians on the opposite shore of the Black Sea.

Yamina had known Hamid first when she was a very little girl, and as the years passed the whole family grew to rely upon him.

When they returned to St. Petersburg it was Hamid who remained to look after the house. He supervised everything and kept the place and the huge staff in readiness for their return.

And it was Hamid now who had carried them away to safety, arranged for Yamina to stay at her father's side on board, and who with consummate cleverness persuaded the Commander of the troopship not to disembark them at the Hospital at Scutari with the other wounded but to take them on to Constantinople.

It necessitated a great deal of argument and exchange of money, but fortunately once again it was Hamid who had brought with them the money which was to prove a life-line in the long months ahead.

Having got them to Constantinople, Hamid found a small house in which they could live.

At first Yamina had been horrified at how small and cramped it was. It looked little more than a white box with a flat roof, like so many other Turkish houses in a poor district.

But she soon realised how wise Hamid had been in choosing nothing pretentious, nothing about which people would ask questions.

What they had to fear was the curiosity of their neighbours and the hunt for spies, which even that first Winter was beginning to make itself felt in the City.

Yamina soon adjusted herself to a life that was so different from anything she had ever known before that sometimes she thought the past must be just a figment of her imagination.

Her father was extremely ill; the Winter added to his weakness by giving him bronchitis, so that he had to sit up in bed and was unable to sleep at night.

As there were only two tiny bed-rooms on the top

floor of the house, divided by a parchment-thin partition, the fact that her father did not sleep but must sit coughing and wheezing all through the long hours of darkness meant that she did not sleep either.

She was also afraid to go out, afraid of meeting people who might ask questions, or of encountering those in authority who would demand to know who they were and where they came from.

It was Hamid who bought not only all the food for the household but also the clothes she needed, having escaped with nothing but what she wore.

Anyway, the elegant and expensive gowns she had worn in the warmth of the Summer months at Balaclava could not have kept out the cold of the Winter and might have betrayed her when she wished to appear unobtrusive and insignificant.

Hamid bought her cheap clothes which were unfashionable but warm, yet even so Yamina could not help endowing them with a grace that made everything she wore become a part of herself.

Her father grew worse, but they did not dare to send for a Physician.

Yamina nursed him as best she could while regretting that she had not studied medicine instead of the many literary subjects which interested both her and her father.

"I am sure the Master will be better when the warmer weather comes," she said to Hamid not once but a thousand times.

And it seemed to her that when the Spring sunshine came through the narrow windows there was a little more colour in her father's cheeks.

Ill though he was, he was still handsome. He had always, Yamina thought, been one of the best-looking men at the Court of St. Petersburg, where handsome men abounded.

Now his hair and his beard had turned white and his eyes were deep-set beneath his high cheek-bones. She thought sometimes when he was asleep that he looked as if he were sculpted in marble.

'Almost as if he lay upon a tomb.'

The thought came to her and like a child she cried out at the agony of it, knowing that to lose her father would be to lose everything in life that remained to her.

Thinking of him now, she left the kitchen which occupied the whole lower half of the house and walked up the narrow, rickety staircase to the upper floor.

The place was sparsely furnished and except for the rugs on the floor, which Hamid had bought in the Bazaar, there were no luxuries of any sort.

Very quietly Yamina opened the door of her father's room.

He lay on a low divan-type bed piled high with pillows so that he could sit upright at night in order to get his breath. Through the windows he could look out over the City below them towards the Bosporus and beyond it to the green hills and mountains.

He was still asleep, Yamina thought as she entered the room, and she moved very softly over the rugs to set down the lime-juice by his bed-side.

'I will not awaken him,' she decided. 'Hamid is right . . . sleep is better medicine than anything I can bring him, and as he has slept so well that perhaps the fever will have passed.'

Having set the jug and glasses down on the table without making a sound, she stood looking down at her father, his straight, aristocratic nose, the square brow from which his white hair was swept back, his closed eyes, and his hands which lay outside the white sheet, relaxed and still.

Yamina was suddenly tense.

Very slowly, as if she forced herself almost against her will, she put out one of her own hands to touch his, and as her fingers felt the cold of his skin, she knew that what she had feared was true.

With a little cry she fell to her knees.

For a moment she could not weep, she could feel

nothing except a sudden cessation of living, as if everything had come to an end.

A long time later, when her eyes had dwelt on his face and she had faced the fact that his spirit had left him and she was alone, she cried out:

"Papa! Papa! How can I manage without you? Oh, my darling, I shall miss you so desperately!"

She could hear her own voice as it were in a vacuum. Then, as if someone told her she must not pray for herself but for her father, she began to say the prayers for the dead.

She had not heard them since her mother's funeral and yet they had remained in her mind so that she could repeat them almost word-perfect.

Only when they were finished and the last "Amen" had left her lips did the tears come, and she bent forward to bury her face against the sheets which covered her father.

* * *

It was a long time later that Yamina went downstairs.

Hamid was waiting for her.

"The Master is dead, Hamid!" she said.

Her voice was steady. There were no longer any tears in her eyes.

"May Allah carry him to Paradise, Mistress."

"He is safe, Hamid. Perhaps that matters more than anything else," Yamina said. "I was afraid, after what we saw today."

"I know, Mistress, and I thought when I came back that perhaps the Master had left us, but I was not sure."

"Supposing that should have . . . happened to . . . him!" Yamina whispered, remembering the spy in the Bazaar.

Then trembling at the thought she said hastily:

"We must be practical, Hamid. If I am discovered, you must not be involved!"

"I will not desert you, Mistress."

"I must leave Constantinople," Yamina said. "But where can I go?"

"I have been thinking, Mistress, for a long time, that this might happen," Hamid said. "I have a suggestion, but you might be angry with me."

"I could never be angry with you, Hamid," Yamina replied. "After all you have done for me, after everything you did for the Master, I shall always be eternally in your debt."

"Then I have been thinking," Hamid said, "that you should go to Mihri until the War is over."

"Mihri?" Yamina exclaimed in amazement. "But Mihri is in the Harem of the Sultan!"

"I know, Mistress, but she has become very important: she is now an *Ikbal*."

Yamina looked surprised.

She knew that an *Ikbal* was an established favourite of the Sultan. Yet when she thought about it, it was not so astonishing; for Mihri had been very beautiful.

A Circassian—and Circassians were the women most sought after and favoured by all Eastern Potentates—Mihri had been abducted from their Estate at Balaclava two years previously.

Yamina had been frantic at the time, furious that such a thing had happened, incensed that one of their own household should have suffered such treatment.

It was, however, impossible to arouse any indignation amongst their other employees or indeed amongst the inhabitants of the Crimea.

It was considered an honour for a girl to be taken to the Seraglio, and anyway, once abducted, there was nothing that could be done even if anyone had wished to protest.

Mihri's family had been employed in Yamina's house in Balaclava ever since it had first been built.

They had asked for work and had proved themselves to be such excellent servants, so honest and efficient, that Yamina had always thought of them as part of the family.

The Circassian women were noted for their beauty all over the East and the hierarchy of the Harem in Constantinople was founded on the law that there should be no liaison between a Sultan and one of his subjects.

Women were therefore always recruited from outside, from Circassia, Georgia, Syria, Rumania, and occasionally a European.

Succeeding Sovereigns therefore were always the sons of slave mothers and only half-Turkish.

Agents of "The Porte," as the Turkish Imperial Government was called, scoured Eastern Europe and the Levant for beautiful girls, and the Circassians ranked first in desirability.

Afterwards Yamina thought that perhaps the beauty of Mihri, which was renowned locally, must somehow have reached the ears of the Agents in Constantinople.

But it was in fact quite usual for raids to be made all along the South coast of Russia, and whatever the families or the authorities might say, it was very well known that the girls themselves were more than willing.

The odalisques were usually well treated, and once they were in the Seraglio there was always the glittering possibility of catching the eye of the Sultan.

The ultimate achievement, if they were beautiful or clever enough, was to become one of his four *Kadins*—or wives—sanctioned by the Prophet.

Every woman dreamed of achieving power, of having the Sultan under her sway, for it was well known that the Monarchs of the Ottoman Empire were all ruled by the women they loved.

After Mihri had been spirited away, Yamina had often thought of her and longed to know how she was faring, besides the fact that she had missed her as a companion and someone young to talk to.

"How could it be possible for me to see Mihri?" she asked Hamid now.

"You will not be angry, Mistress, but Mihri knows that you are here."

"She does? But how can that be?"

"You remember Sahin?" Hamid enquired.

Yamina thought for a moment.

"But of course. He also was kidnapped by the Agents of the Sultan. I remember my father talking about him and being very angry, but I was young at the time, only ten years old."

"Sahin became a White Eunuch!" Hamid said.

"A eunuch?"

There was a note of horror in Yamina's voice.

Her father had told her that the practise of employing eunuchs was not adopted until the middle of the fifteenth century.

"Despotism and polygamy," he explained, "created the necessity for eunuchs."

Later she learnt that the supplying of unfortunate boys to satisfy the demand of the Turks for eunuch guards was a trade in itself.

Few survived the operation, from which they were left to recover or die, buried up to their waists in the burning sands.

White Eunuchs, like white female slaves from Circassia or Greece, fetched high prices.

"Sahin is also powerful," Hamid said, "but not as powerful as Mihri; for White Eunuchs have no longer the power of the Black."

"You have seen Sahin?"

"I have seen him, Mistress, and because I can trust him I told him where we were and he has told Mihri."

Yamina sat down in a chair, but her eyes were on Hamid's face.

"Mihri says come to her. She keep you safe and hide you until peace come."

Hamid paused. He saw that Yamina's eyes were wide with astonishment.

She could hardly believe that what she was hearing was true. Then with a helpless gesture Hamid added:

"There is no-one else. No-where for you to go, Mistress, and there is only a little money left."

Yamina drew in her breath.

When they had first escaped from Balaclava it had seemed to her that the money Hamid had brought with them would be enough to last for years.

But during the War food had become expensive. There had also been the expensive luxuries she had been forced to purchase for her father.

He had never drunk anything but the best wine, and sometimes when his breathing was not troubling him he would long for a cigar.

All these things seemed ridiculously unimportant when Yamina remembered how much they had spent in the past in their magnificent house with over one hundred servants to wait on them and another hundred in the gardens outside.

But what money they had with them when they escaped had been in Russian currency, and it had been difficult to change it.

Hamid had managed to do so only by pretending that he had stolen it on the battlefield or obtained it in the past when trading with a people who were not the enemy.

Naturally he did not get a good rate of exchange, and Yamina had often wondered how long it would be before the real enemy of which they must be afraid was starvation.

Now she had to face facts.

It would be impossible for her and Hamid to try to reach some other country without money.

It would be equally impossible for them to return to Russia.

She had thought once or twice that perhaps, if her father died, she would be able to get back to Russia and find her way to St. Petersburg. But she knew now that it would be impossible without a considerable sum of money to bribe a boatman to carry her across the Black Sea.

But to enter a Harem!

Every instinct in her body shrank from the idea.

"You will be safe, Mistress," Hamid said, as if he knew where her thoughts were taking her, "and Sahin says that later they will somehow get you away. It is not as difficult as it was when the Sultan lived in the Seraglio. Now he is at the Dolmabahce Palace, which is on the shore of the Bosporus. Perhaps one night there could be a boat. Mihri is clever and she has great power."

"But the . . . Harem!" Yamina murmured.

"Sahin say Mihri will pretend you her sister."

Yamina got to her feet and walked across the kitchen to stand at the open window.

Outside, the sunshine was still brilliant on the flat roofs of the white houses, but the afternoon was drawing to a close. Soon night would fall—the soft velvet night of the Levant with great stars shining like diamonds in the sky.

There would be lights too on the Bosporus, the lights of the steamships moving into the Black Sea, carrying more men to fight against the Russians who were still holding out at Sebastopol.

Soldiers who sooner or later, Yamina thought clairvoyantly, would pierce the defences so that Sebastopol would fall and the Russians be humiliated.

Then at last there would be peace; but until then she was in danger—deadly danger.

When the house-to-house search began, she would be discovered. She had no papers, nothing to prove her identity, and she was quite certain that confronted with a Frenchman, the subterfuge she had used on Lord Castleford would be ineffective.

She might appear genuinely French to an Englishman or to a Turk, but certainly not to a Frenchman.

Yet everything she had ever heard about the Sultan's Harem, the secrecy, the mystery, and the crimes that took place there, seemed to close in on her like a nightmare of horror.

"Always since I have been in Constantinople", she thought. "I have been conscious of the Seraglio, now empty for two years, standing dark against the skyline."

Although it had been a town in itself, housing several thousand persons and containing everything within its sacred precincts from wood-cutters to musicians, from astrologers to apothecaries, dwarfs and buffoons to the Keeper of the Parrot-Cages, it was now still, peopled only by ghosts, terrifying.

How could a woman not think of all the whispered rumours about the Seraglio of the *bostanjis*—the gardener–boatmen who sewed any woman who was unfaithful or had displeased the Sultan into a weighted sack and drowned her in Seraglio Point?

They died in the presence of the Black Eunuchs who supervised them in death as they had done in life.

To the Christian world, the Sultans in Constantinople were looked upon as monsters of licentiousness and sin.

Although Yamina was too well educated and too intelligent not to know that the present Sultan, under the influence of the British Ambassador, was an intelligent man who had carried out a large number of reforms, there was still in the background the mystery of his private life.

Her father had often explained to her that the Turkish passion for concealment amounted to a fetish.

Their homes, their women, and their Monarch were all shrouded in mystery not only from foreigners but also from one another.

"It is typical," he had said, "that when the Sultan rides abroad in his Capital he is surrounded by guards who carry banners and pearl-fringed umbrellas, and even wear helmets topped by waving ostrich-plumes so as to screen their Master from curious eyes."

"Why are the Turks like that?" Yamina had asked with interest.

"It is bred deep into their character," her father replied. "That is why so many legends are told about the cruelty and the crimes perpetrated inside the Seraglio. Some may be true, but I am prepared to believe that a large number of them are invented."

"Will we ever know the truth?" Yamina enquired.

"It is unlikely," he answered. "I believe the British Ambassador has persuaded the Sultan recently to change much of his protocol. In the past the foreign visitors he received were first submitted to a ritual bath."

"A bath!" Yamina cried.

"As you know, the Moslems are fanatical about cleanliness." Her father smiled. "So, having been cleansed before entering the sacred precincts, visitors were then clothed in magnificent robes and lifted bodily into the presence of the Sultan, supported on each side by Court dignitaries."

"But why?" Yamina asked.

Her father had laughed.

"I suppose the overwhelming honour might have paralysed them!"

"What happened then?" she enquired curiously.

"I have been told by those who visited the Sultan that they were vouchsafed one jewelled finger, extended through the drawn curtains of the throne."

"Curtains?" Yamina asked.

"I will show you a picture of it," her father replied. "It is like a gigantic four-poster bed with a framework of silver gilt and encrusted with a dazzling array of precious stones, emeralds, rubies the size of hens' eggs, and its brocade hangings were, of course, stiff with pearls and gold."

Because of the stories her father told her, Yamina had found herself extremely interested in the Seraglio and the women who were immured there.

Their numbers, she learnt, exceeded three hundred but that was not to say that the estimate was accurate. No-one knew exactly how many were incarcerated in the Sultan's Harem.

And now, although it seemed incredible, Hamid was suggesting that she should enter the place of which someone had once said:

"Religion is pleasure and God the Sultan!"

"I cannot do it . . . I cannot!" she whispered to herself.

And yet what was the alternative? To wait until the Turkish authorities, or, more terrifying, a mob, arrived to drag her from her hiding-place? To run away into the open country and there starve to death?

To throw herself on the mercy of the British?

She knew, although she would hardly admit it to herself, that she would be treated with courtesy, and perhaps generosity, if she went to the Ambassador and told him the position in which she found herself.

But in fact what could he do but hand her over to the Turkish authorities?

She would be imprisoned, if she was not executed as a spy.

"I really have very little choice in the matter," Yamina told herself.

Yet once again she trembled at the thought of going to Mihri and being shut up in the most terrifying, the most notorious, and the most talked-about prison in the world.

The Harem of the "Shadow of Allah Upon Earth, The Prophet's Successor, The Master of Masters."

She realised that Hamid was waiting for her to speak and she felt renewed gratitude and affection for the man who had risked so much and who had remained loyal to them even though the country of her and her father was in fact at war with his.

"Why have you done this for us, Hamid?" she asked, following the train of her thoughts.

"You made your home my home," Hamid answered. "The Master and you, Mistress, are my people."

It was said simply and with all sincerity and Yamina felt the tears come into her eyes.

"What can we do about the Master, Hamid?" she asked helplessly. "He must be buried, but where? How can we try to find a Priest without betraying ourselves?"

"I think, Mistress," Hamid answered, "when you go we burn house!"

Yamina gave a startled exclamation, but after her first impulse of horror she realised it was the sensible thing to do.

Apart from her own natural desire that her father should be buried in consecrated ground, there was Hamid to consider.

If he was found to have hidden and served two Russians, his life would be immediately forfeited.

Besides, something perhaps Oriental in Yamina's blood reacted to the suggestion of a funeral pyre!

It was what her father might appreciate, she thought. He had often complained that death was gloomy and funerals morbid.

Once, many years ago, he had said to her:

"I hate the idea of being put in a hole in the ground, and when I saw my father's coffin deposited in the family vault I thought that was equally unpleasant. Yet what is the alternative?"

It had been a passing thought, but now the memory of it came back to her and Yamina knew she had the answer.

She and Hamid would set fire to the house and the flames would leap up towards the sky. There would be nothing left of her father's body but ashes and there would be no hole in the ground, no gloomy vault where he was concerned.

"You are right, Hamid," she said aloud. "That is what we must do."

"Mistress permit, I go now and make arrangements with Sahin. Do not open door until I return."

"Go, and Allah go with you," Yamina said, giving the familiar blessing of the East, and for a moment Hamid's grave face was lit with a smile.

"One day, Mistress, we will go home."

"I am sure of that! But whatever happens to me, Hamid," Yamina said, "you must go back, and when my relatives come from St. Petersburg, My Uncle or his sons . . . my cousins, to discover what has happened, tell them what you did for the Master and me."

Hamid bowed and made the obeisance that comes naturally to an Easterner when he is moved. Then without saying any more he went from the house, closing the door behind him.

When she was alone Yamina put her hands up to her face.

She could not credit that the conversation she had just had with Hamid had actually taken place.

Had she really committed herself to take refuge in the Sultan's Palace, to hide in his Harem?

And yet she knew that if she could be safe anywhere she could be safe with Mihri.

The beautiful Circassian was a year older than Yamina and had been at the height of her beauty when she had been taken away by the Sultan's Agents.

Only after everyone on the Estate had searched for her for three days did they learn the truth and realise where she had gone.

While Yamina had cried bitterly at the thought of losing someone she loved, she was well aware that the other women in the house were smiling. When they talked about Mihri they said that it was fitting that she should be in the one place where her beauty would be appreciated.

It was her father who had made Yamina see that for Mihri, like so many other girls, it was the chance of a life-time.

"How could she bear it?" Yamina had said passionately. "To be one of three hundred others, to have to pray and hope that she will attract the Sultan's attention, yet knowing how heavily the odds were against her! And even if he does notice her, the others will be jealous, hating her for being preferred."

"I have a feeling that women are much the same the world over," her father answered with a smile. "They all want to attract the attention of men, and in every country they hope to make an advantageous marriage. For Mihri to become an *Ikbal,* one who has caught the Royal eye, will, I am quite sure, be the summit of her ambition in life."

"Mihri is intelligent," Yamina retorted angrily. "I taught her to read and write. She can speak a little English, her French is good, and I suppose now she will have learnt Turkish."

"She would find it difficult to communicate with a large number of people in the Harem unless she does so," her father replied. "But the Sultan speaks both French and English, so where he is concerned she will find herself at an advantage over many of her rivals."

"I doubt if any of them will be as beautiful as Mihri," Yamina said hotly.

She knew now that she had been right.

If Mihri was an *Ikbal*—an established favourite—there was always the chance that sooner or later she might become a *Kadin,* or wife of the Sultan, and what Eastern woman could ask for more?

As an *Ikbal* Mihri must now have a certain amount of power, and that meant that she could ensure her safety from persecution not only in the Harem but at the hands of the Sultan himself.

There would be no other man to trouble her, Yamina thought, and she was well aware that if it came to a competition with a Circassian she would not, in Turkish eyes, be thought to have a chance.

Mihri's fair hair and white skin were everything that an Eastern Potentate would find alluring.

"I shall be safe in more ways than one!" Yamina told herself reassuringly.

Then, as if she could not bear to contemplate it any longer, she went upstairs to kneel once again beside her father in prayer.

Hamid did not return until very late.

Yamina was downstairs waiting for him, having cooked a meal for them both simply because she felt she must do something and found it difficult to sit patiently waiting.

When he came in through the door she jumped to her feet to look at him apprehensively, wondering frantically what he had to tell her.

He made her his usual courteous obeisance before he said:

"All is well, Mistress!"

"You have let Mihri know that the Master is . . . dead?"

"I have seen Sahin. He spoke to her while I waited. She will send a chair for you tomorrow and Sahin will ensure that you can enter the Palace, and that no-one will speak with you until you are taken to Mihri herself."

There was silence, then after a moment Yamina said:

"There is . . . nothing else I can do . . . is there, Hamid?"

"Nothing, Mistress, and I know this will be best. Already there are more riots in the City and more spies have been executed."

There was a note in his voice which told Yamina that he too had found it horrifying.

"You are quite certain," she said after a moment, "that when the War is over I shall be able to leave?"

"Mihri will arrange it, and Sahin has promised me that somehow they will get you away."

'If they cannot do so,' Yamina thought to herself, 'I must die. It is not the worst thing that can happen to anyone, and rather than be a prisoner in a gilded cage for the rest of my life I will join Papa, wherever he may be.'

The long hours she had sat upstairs at her father's bed-side had brought her a strange peace.

At first she had wanted only to cry at the loss of him. Then she began to feel as though he were beside her, comforting her, telling her that what happened to the body was of no importance; it was the spirit, the soul, that mattered.

In the years after her mother's death Yamina had grown very close to her father.

He had been a clever, cultured man with a great many interests, but most of all he had enjoyed reading history, delving into the past, telling her about civilisations that had existed in other ages.

Once when they had been talking about the great Genghis Khan and about Alexander the Great Yamina had said with a sigh:

"It seemed such a waste! All they achieved, all they fought for, is lost and forgotten! It died with them, so what was the point of all their efforts?"

Her father had smiled.

"Nothing is lost, my child," he answered. "Every ounce of human endeavour goes back into the great Force from which it has come. It is Life which activates us all."

"To further effort?" Yamina enquired. "To more achievement?"

"Exactly!" he replied.

"And then we too are lost!"

"Not lost, merely reactivated, because that is the whole point of evolution. It goes on. Great figures evolve, but they in their turn give way to others."

He had paused before saying:

"I believe that everything we do, everything we think, contributes to the whole, so that nothing is wasted."

Yamina had tried to understand, but she had been too young at the time.

Later she had thought how the Seasons came and went, the seed and leaf from a tree went back into the soil, only to create other trees and other leaves.

'Perhaps we are the same,' she thought to herself, 'in which case there is no death, but only rebirth.'

That was the message she was sure her father was trying to give her.

Yet it was hard to think of anything now save her immediate predicament, and the decision she had to make, which might mean the end of her life since if she could never get away there would be nothing for her to look forward to except death.

"What am I to do, Hamid?" she asked with a sudden feeling of terror.

"You have always been brave, Mistress," he answered, "like the Master. You both have great courage."

That was the right reply, Yamina thought.

It was courage she needed now, courage which could take her on this strange adventure to which she could not see the end. Yet she had the feeling that she was not entirely alone.

She would be sustained and helped if not by her father by someone who had saved them from falling into the hands of the enemy at Balaclava, who had brought them in safety to Constantinople.

That Someone or Something had also enabled them to live for six months together and content, even though they were deprived of the luxuries to which they were accustomed, or even the comfort of security.

'I have not been unhappy these six months,' Yamina thought to herself and knew it was true.

There had been a strange happiness in the comradeship which united her father, Hamid, and herself.

There had been a feeling that they were protected and that Someone greater than themselves was caring for them.

She could not explain it, and yet it had been there.

They had not harmed anyone, they hurt no-one, and their hearts were certainly not at war.

They only wanted peace, and so mentally they had found peace in this uncomfortable little Turkish house hidden in the enemy Capital.

They had no friends, no-one to turn to but themselves, and yet, against all odds, they had survived up to this moment.

"Now I have to face the future alone," Yamina told herself, and knew that that was why it was more frightening then anything she had experienced in the past.

When she entered the Harem, she would find herself without the support of her father and of Hamid, on which she had always relied.

It was like starting out on a dangerous voyage, not knowing her final destination, knowing for sure nothing but the fact that she would be . . . alone.

Chapter 3

Yamina came down the staircase into the kitchen where Hamid was waiting for her.

She was wearing the basic garments of every Turkish woman and the long loose sleeves of her *entari* fell back from the gauze sleeves of her chemise.

On her legs were the *Salvar,* or wide trousers, caught at the ankle. Her hair was unbound and she wore the traditional *talpock,* a small, flat, round tasselled cap, a little on one side of her head.

"Do I look all right?" she asked Hamid.

He looked her over carefully before he replied gravely:

"You are quite correct, Mistress!"

Yamina was aware as she dressed that Mihri had sent her only cheap, ordinary garments such as might be expected of a girl coming from a poor Circassian home. She was sure that when she reached the Harem there would be different clothes awaiting her.

She felt strange as she put them on and completed the whole ensemble with the small, embroidered Turkish slippers which turned up at the toes.

There was a veil to be worn over her face, and over everything else a black *ferejeh,* which every Turkish woman wore in the streets.

There was however no question of Yamina walking to the Dolmabahce Palace.

A Sedan chair carried by two black deaf mutes had been sent for her—a precaution, Yamina knew, so that they could never say from where she had come.

Hamid was to escort the chair in which she travelled to the gateway of the Palace, and after that he would leave her in Sahin's hands, who would deliver her to Mihri.

That much she knew; but it was little enough and it made her feel as if already she had set the wheels of some gigantic machine in motion and now she must be propelled forward by it into the unknown.

As she stood in the kitchen with Hamid's eyes on her Turkish garments Yamina thought how strange her life had become. This time last year she had expected nothing more eventful than the journey to and back from the Crimea to St. Petersburg.

She thought of the social life, Balls, Receptions, and Assemblies which took place in the Russian Capital, and the quiet peacefulness of the beautiful gardens of their Summer home that stretched down to the Black Sea.

Now, in the course of a few months, she had been involved in the War, escaped to the Capital of her country's enemies, and now was preparing to enter the Harem of the dreaded "Shadow of the Prophet Mohammed"!

It all seemed incredible, and yet it was actually happening!

"Are you ready, Mistress?" Hamid asked.

She knew by the expression in his eyes that he

was feeling anxious, as she was, about what the future might hold.

"I must say good-bye to the Master," Yamina replied.

She went upstairs again, leaving her veil and her *ferejeh* on the kitchen table.

She had drawn the curtains in her father's room but there were four lighted candles at the four corners of the bed.

He looked like the stone sculpture on a tomb. His hands were crossed over his chest and on the sheets which covered him there was a bunch of lilies-of-the-valley which Hamid had bought in the Bazaar. The fragrance of them made Yamina remember the times they had walked together in the gardens he had created, where the scent of flowers had filled the air.

Now, though dead and far from home, he still had a magnificence about him.

He had accepted the change in their circumstances as all through his life he had accepted with a philosophical calm whatever fate might bring.

He had never complained, he had never railed against the injustice of being involved in a war which did not concern him personally.

He had tried in his own way to transmit to Yamina some of his faith in all that was highest and best.

"It is our intellect that serves us in times of adversity," he said to her once. "It is our brain that gives us courage and the strength to overcome fear. That is of more importance than anything else."

Her father had never been afraid, Yamina thought, and as she knelt down beside his bed she wondered if at this moment he was fearful for her, while he would never have shrunk from anything he had to suffer personally.

"Help me, Papa, to be like you!" she prayed. "Give me courage if I must die, to face it without screaming, without losing my self-control."

It was a prayer that came from her heart, a prayer that she knew was fundamentally what her father would have expected of her in all circumstances, however horrifying.

Then even as she prayed she saw again the blood-stained face of the Russian spy being dragged through the Bazaar, and wondered if he had screamed and struggled when they had first pulled him from his hiding-place.

Perhaps he had been the stuff of which martyrs were made, who went to their deaths with smiles on their faces, defying those who executed them.

"Could I be like that?" Yamina asked herself, and her thoughts shied away from the answer.

"Help me, Papa! Help me!" she prayed.

Once again she said the prayers for the dead that had been said over her mother's coffin.

But here there could be no Service and no Priest.

Her father had not been able to receive the Last Rites of the Church and yet she felt that it would not matter in the "Great To-Be" where she was sure he was at this moment, safe and free from pain.

She said the last words of the Burial-Service.

"*Requiescat in pace*. Amen."

Then she rose to her feet, crossing herself as she did so, to stand looking down for the last time at the father she had loved and who had loved her.

They had been so close during the last years of his life, and while they had been hidden away in this small Turkish house, Yamina thought, they had been closer than at any other time.

Sometimes there had been no need for talk, for they had known what the other was thinking.

Often, as their minds explored subjects in which they both were interested, they would forget where they were and be carried away into the past, to the Byzantine Empire, to the mysteries of China or the days of the Pharaohs.

"Who will talk to me about such things now?" Yamina wondered wistfully.

Then, realising that time was passing, she took one last look at her father's face, until blinded with tears she turned away to descend to the kitchen.

Hamid held her veil in his hands and without speaking he covered her face with it, then put over her shoulders the black *ferejeh.*

"Will you wait, Mistress?" he asked.

Yamina nodded, unable to speak.

Hamid went up the stairs and she heard him moving about on the floor above and knew that he was pouring the petroleum-oil he had bought in the Bazaar over the floor so that it encircled the bed.

He came downstairs again and now he poured from the can he carried in his hands the same oil over the kitchen floor, the furniture, and the walls.

Finally, still without speaking, he opened the door and Yamina went outside.

The Sedan chair sent from the Harem was waiting. It looked not unlike those which were used in Britain to carry old ladies at Brighton or in St. Petersburg by those who could not afford a *drozhki.*

The deaf mutes averted their eyes as Hamid helped Yamina into it, and the red curtains were pulled tightly so it was impossible for any passer-by to see whom the chair contained.

The mutes would have picked up the shafts, but Hamid made a gesture signifying "wait" and went back into the house.

Peeping through the curtains, Yamina knew what he was about to do and held her breath.

After a few seconds she saw the first leaping flame of the fire Hamid had kindled, crimson and gold, through the glass of the downstairs windows. A second later he came from the house, closing the door behind him.

He walked to the chair and gave a sign for the mutes to lift it off the ground and start shuffling down the hill.

At that moment the oil with which Hamid had covered the floor ignited and tongues of flame came through the sides of the windows and beneath the door.

The deaf mutes turned their heads as if in surprise before, at Hamid's command, they moved away.

Looking back, Yamina could see the flames leaping now from the upper windows and appearing to come out of the very roof itself.

Higher and higher, stronger and stronger, the fire burned until even when they were some distance away she could hear the roar of it and the flames seemed to light the whole neighbourhood.

People came hurrying up the road and out of the houses to see what was happening.

By this time they were almost out of sight and Yamina shut the curtains, determined that she would look no more.

And yet, almost involuntarily, as she felt the Sedan chair now moving more swiftly down the road which inclined towards the City, she leaned forward to have one last look.

Her view was obscured by some cypress trees, and yet through their dark branches she could see the red glow.

In a way, she thought, it was a splendid funeral pyre, which would have appealed to her father's imagination.

"You died in a blaze of glory, Papa," she wanted to say to him, and almost felt as though he could hear her and that he chuckled in response.

Then as she would have closed the curtains once again to sit back in the semi-darkness inside the box-like chair, she glanced down the road and saw riding towards them a man on a horse.

She recognised Lord Castleford immediately.

There was no-one else she had seen since she came to Constantinople who looked like him.

It was not only his elegant riding-clothes, which reminded her of the men she had known in St. Petersburg, it was also the way he carried his head with a kind of arrogance about it.

Only an Englishman, she thought, could look so aloof, so utterly indifferent to his surroundings.

And yet she had to admit that riding a well-bred animal, such as the one on which he had carried her when they had escaped from the Bazaar, he looked very distinguished.

As she drew nearer to him she wondered why in fact he was on this particular road in an unimportant, poor part of the City. Then she was sure she could guess the answer.

Could he be looking for her? Could he still be persistent in his intention to call on her, which she had very ably prevented him from doing?

Perhaps Lord Castleford thought he might catch a glimpse of her. Or was she just imagining his interest, and by this time had he forgotten the woman he had helped to escape from an unpleasant situation?

They were drawing nearer when Yamina had a sudden impulse to call out to him.

Supposing, she thought to herself, she asked for his assistance? Supposing she told him her predicament, that she was in fact Russian, though certainly not a spy?

Would he help her? Was there any chance of his doing so?

Even as she thought of it, Yamina knew the idea was absurd.

What could Lord Castleford, staying at the British Embassy, do but hand her over immediately to the Turkish authorities?

As a Diplomat and as a guest of the Great Elchi, it would be unthinkable that he should do anything but behave correctly.

Now Yamina could hear the sound of his horse's hoofs. They had drawn level. Perhaps he would recognise Hamid!

She held her breath.

Then she knew that it was unlikely that Lord Castleford, so superciliously indifferent to his surroundings, would give an ordinary Turk walking by the side of a Sedan chair a second glance.

There was nothing to distinguish Hamid from the thousands of other Turks, who were similarly dressed and looked, especially to a foreigner, almost identical.

They were past.

The sound of his horse's hoofs was fading into the distance and Yamina closed the curtains and sat back.

He could not help her. Nobody could! What must be must be! That was the fatalism of the East and she must accept it for herself.

* * *

Afterwards Yamina could hardly remember her first sight of the magnificent white marble gateway of the Dolmabahce Palace.

She was to learn later that it represented a mixture of Turkish and European architecture and that to the Sultan it was everything that was modern and desirable.

The vast pile covering a great acreage of land, with the Bosporus flowing on one side and backed by verdant parks and hills, was a fairy-like edifice compared with the dark, gloomy, and ancient Seraglio.

Two enormous wings were attached to the *corps-de-logis,* and before the broad white steps leading from the front of the Palace to the water's edge a Royal Caique waited, ready to carry the Sultan across the waves to whatever other part of his domain he fancied.

No-one, Yamina was to think later, could imagine a more beautiful or more suitable vehicle for a Sultan.

Spotlessly white with borders of rose-colour and gold, she watched it from a lattice-window ride on the water, light as a butterfly.

Twelve rowers, clad in white Bronssa silk with scarlet fezes, dipped their gold-tipped oars. At the stern, a dome of crimson velvet supported on gold colonnettes held a silk divan on which the Caliph could recline.

An Arab with draperies of scarlet and gold held the helm and a golden eagle with out-stretched wings guarded the poop.

But this was all part of the beauty, the luxury, and the splendour of Dolmabahce Palace.

First, as she was taken through the great main gate and knew that Hamid must be left behind, Yamina had a moment of panic and thought she must rise from the chair and run back into the streets before the great gates closed upon her.

She heard the murmur of voices but was too frightened even to look through the curtain for fear of what she would see.

Then she heard Hamid's voice say quietly:

"Allah be with you, Mistress—we shall meet again."

He spoke in a manner that was prophetic and Yamina longed to believe him.

But how could they meet again? How would she ever see him? she wondered. Dear Hamid, who had been so kind and helpful, who had saved her father from being captured by the British and both of them from being imprisoned by the Turks.

Last night she had said to him:

"Perhaps when there is peace, if I have not been able to escape from the Harem, my relatives can buy my freedom."

Even as she spoke she knew it was a forlorn hope. What money could her family offer which would be of any interest to a Sultan? And who had ever heard of anyone who had once entered the gates of the Harem returning from behind its locked doors?

But it was too late to tell her fears to Hamid, and she was only glad that she could leave him enough money to live on until he could find work.

"Do not worry, Mistress," Hamid begged her. "With the War there are a hundred different jobs I can get tomorrow. Young men are fighting, the old ones must take their place."

Yamina knew this was true. Everywhere in Constantinople there were notices offering employment to workmen of every sort and description, and Hamid was a skilled man.

"I also have relatives in Constantinople," Hamid said. "They have not seen me for some years, but the blood-tie is there. I can stay with them until I find employment."

Hamid was taken care of, Yamina thought, and now she had only herself to worry about.

She was taken to a side door of the Palace, where the chair was set down and the curtains pulled back.

It was then that she saw Sahin! She had not seen him since she was a child and for a moment she found it hard to recognise him.

He still had the handsome features that she had never forgotten, his skin was still white, his hair fair; but like all eunuchs he had grown fat and it was hard to remember the slim, athletic boy who had been abducted from their Estate nine years ago.

Sahin made her a slight obeisance, then beckoning her he took her along a narrow passage and up a staircase which Yamina could see through her veil looked quite ordinary.

Then they reached what she knew must be the door of the Harem.

The locks and hinges were superior examples of the metalsmith's craft. Made of bronze, they were damascened with gold and silver, and the key, which a Black Eunuch brought from his belt at the sight of Yamina, was of gold encrusted with jewels.

As he turned it in the lock, Sahin faded away into the shadows; for the White Eunuchs were not allowed into the Holy of Holies, the Harem itself.

Conscious that her heart was beating violently against her breast and her lips felt dry, Yamina waited. Then suddenly walking towards her there came a man who she knew was the Chief Black Eunuch, the Kizlar Aga.

All she had read about the Sultan's household made Yamina aware that he was by far the most important person in the new world she was entering alone and unprotected.

The Kizlar Aga's power was absolute. He alone had the right to speak directly to the Sultan. He was at once Comptroller of the Household, Master of Ceremonies, and the Sultan's confidant.

He was in supreme control of the Harem and the odalisques and in his hands lay the power of life and death.

He was entitled to have both eunuchs and girls as slaves for himself, and was allotted as many as three hundred horses for his own use.

The Kizlar Aga was so large that he seemed almost to waddle rather than walk.

He wore a pelisse of red. His hat was like a huge white sugar-loaf, worn on a slant at the back of his head.

He did not speak, but his eyes flickered over Yamina in an insolent manner before he turned to lead her through several large rooms in which she could see cushions of sumptuous silks, stools and hangings of velvet worked in gold thread and set with precious stones, while the carpets of Ghiordes, Bergamo, or Melés were the perfection of Turkish artistry.

But Yamina had little time to observe anything before she was shown into a room where there was only one woman, and with a little exclamation of relief she saw that it was Mihri holding out her arms.

She ran towards the Circassian, and as they embraced the door shut behind them and Yamina realised that the Black Eunuch had left them alone.

"Mihri! Mihri!" she exclaimed. "How glad I am to see you!"

"And I you!" Mihri replied.

She glanced towards the door, then bent low over Yamina's hand and kissed it.

"Forgive me," she said in a very low voice, "but I embraced you because here they believe you to be my sister. It was the only way I could be sure that they would let you come to me."

"I am only too glad to be your sister," Yamina assured her.

"Then you will understand that I must address you by your name," Mihri said. "They would think it strange if I address you in terms of respect as I did in the past."

"You must take no risks," Yamina said quickly. "What would they do to you, Mihri, if they thought you had deceived them?"

Mihri gave her an enigmatic smile and Yamina thought she was even more beautiful than she had been two years ago.

Her *entari* was buttoned by huge diamonds and belted by a wide, heavy girdle which was a mosaic of precious stones.

The stomacher-clasp was fashioned with enormous diamonds and huge egg-shaped pearls.

Her feet were bare and tinted with henna. On her head she wore a *talpock* studded with pearls.

Pinned to her hair there was a large *aigrette* of diamonds, springing from a brooch designed to represent a bouquet of ruby roses, pearl buds, emerald leaves, and diamond stems.

Her long blonde hair was left unbound and it fell over her shoulders glittering with diamonds which were attached to fine gold chains.

Mihri's lips were crimson, her eyes darkened by kohl, and her eye-brows were like ebony wings against the whiteness of her skin.

She looked so lovely that Yamina could only stare at her as Mihri drew her down to sit on one of the low velvet-covered sofas set against the walls of marble lattice-work, so delicate it might have been made of lace.

Mihri smiled.

"You are looking for the little servant-girl who used to mend your clothes," she said. "Now everything is changed."

"I hear you are of great importance," Yamina said.

"I am an *Ikbal*," Mihri replied, "and the Sultan

loves me. Soon, I think very soon, I shall become a *Kadin.*"

"He is kind to you?" Yamina enquired.

"He is my Lord and my Master and I worship at his feet," Mihri replied.

There was a note in her voice that told Yamina that she was not exaggerating. Then, like women all over the world, she could not help boasting.

"Look at my jewels!" she said. "My bracelets, my rings, the diamonds round my neck! There is nothing —nothing he will not give me!"

"I am so glad, Mihri," Yamina said. "But you should not have risked losing his favour for me."

"I have never forgotten your kindness," Mihri said, "nor that of your mother, the most beautiful lady I ever saw!"

As she spoke she put her fingers to her lips and looked over her shoulder.

"People are always listening," she whispered. "I must remember to say '*our* mother,' '*our* life together.' My past must be your past, otherwise they will be suspicious."

"I will be very careful," Yamina promised.

Mihri looked at her and her eyes sparkled.

"Come," she said. "We must dress you as befits the sister of an *Ikbal,* and you must look beautiful."

She paused to add:

"But not too beautiful! If you catch the eye of the Sultan, then I shall hate you!"

"I think that is unlikely, when he can look at you." Yamina smiled.

She was to learn in the next few days of the fierce jealousies that raged in the Harem.

The first thing that surprised her was that those who had imagined it was a temple of unbridled licence had never known of the strict formality that existed.

It was a hierarchy with its own protocol and etiquette, and, as many of the odalisques never even saw the Sultan, they were forced to spend their whole lives inventing ways of passing the time.

Looking round her with curious eyes, Yamina saw how unnatural existence within the Harem could be.

All the women lived for the chance of catching the Sultan's eye. If they failed in this, they were forced to console themselves with over-eating, sweet-meat making, the playing of musical instruments, embroidery, or the distraction of strange, unnatural love-affairs with one another.

Because the Sultan had concentrated his affections on Mihri, Yamina was not able to see what happened when he paid a State visit to his Harem.

But Mihri and the others were only too eager to explain to her what occurred.

First of all, a new-comer to the Harem had to attend a school—which Yamina described to herself as an "*Académie de l'Amour*" where they were instructed in the art of love.

They must learn to approach "Allah's Shadow on Earth" with humility, crawling into the Imperial bed from the foot, inching up slowly.

This was their chance, the supreme moment for which they had waited and prayed.

But in the back of their minds there must always have been the memory of many failures and of Sultans like Ibrahim who required twenty-four virgins in as many hours.

Or there was Sultan Selim III, a gentle young Prince, who was so horrified at the custom of strangling every infant born in the Seraglio who was not the child of the reigning Sultan that he decided never to risk becoming a father!

But in contrast to these fears, the history of the Ottoman Empire was a long testimony to the enormous power wielded by women in the Harem.

Cruel, cunning, ruthless, ambitious, many of the *Kadins* enslaved their Lord and Master and ruled not only the Seraglio but also the country.

When they had been taught all they should know, the odalisques had to pass what to all intents and purposes was an Examining Board, usually presided over by the Sultan's mother, known as the "*Sultan Valideh.*"

Nothing was left to chance, and as Mihri said in a practical tone:

"It saves the 'Master of Masters' many disappointments!"

When the new-comer was pronounced perfect in the oldest art in the world, she passed into the ranks of the ladies-in-waiting, joining at least two or three hundred more, all voluptuous, jealous, and bored, all specialised in the art they could so seldom practise, all waiting for their great chance.

This came when the Sultan paid them a State visit.

He was announced by the eunuchs who rang a great golden bell.

This was followed by a feverish rush for the most elaborate and spectacular clothes.

Faces were painted, lips were crimsoned, and eyes darkened to look mysterious and alluring.

The Chief Treasurer of the Harem, together with the *Sultan Valideh*, received the Sultan in State at the entrance to the Harem and conducted him with the Chief Eunuch to the Reception held either in the apartments of the Sultan's mother or in those of his reigning favourite.

"It is very exciting!" Mihri explained. "A eunuch walks first, magnificently dressed and chanting:

" 'Behold our Sovereign! Emperor of the True Believers, Shadow of Allah Upon Earth, The Prophet's Successor, Master of Masters, Chosen Among the Chosen, our Padishah, our Sultan! Long live our Sultan! Let us admire Him who is the glory of the House of Osman'!"

"What happens then?" Yamina asked.

"The Sultan passes through the ranks of women," Mihri answered. "Everyone holds herself in the prescribed pose, the head thrown back, the hands across the breast."

"Who is there?" Yamina enquired.

"Everybody!" Mihri answered. "Past favourites, the family, the daughters, or Sultanas, the *Kadins*, or wives by whom the Sultan has had children, the *Ikbals* who have already enjoyed the Royal attention, and the *Guzdehs*."

"What are those?" Yamina asked.

"They who have caught the Sultan's eye but have not yet been tried by him."

She went on to explain how at such a ceremony everyone was offered silver trays of coffee and sweetmeats, while the odalisques clustered round the Sultan, feverishly making every effort to attract his attention.

"And he chose you!" Yamina smiled.

"He chose me!" Mihri agreed.

"How?" Yamina asked.

"He asked the *Valideh Sultan* my name. I was then authorised to approach the dais and kiss the cushion of the Master's divan."

"And after he sent for you?"

"We have been very happy, more happy than I could have believed possible. And if, as I think, I am to have a child, then he has promised to take me as his wife, his *Kadin!*"

She gave a little sigh of satisfaction and added:

"Then I shall have larger rooms, more slaves, more jewels, and more money!"

Yamina could not help wondering whether this counted more than the Sultan himself, but she was too wise to say so.

Abdul Medjid, she had learnt, possessed none of his father's personality. His good qualities—a kind disposition and a sense of duty—were overshadowed by his lack of vigour.

In appearance he was short, thin, and pale. He was, Yamina heard, often melancholy, but his face lit up when he smiled.

He had already reigned for sixteen years, a phenomenally long time in the history of the Ottoman Empire. Sultans invariably died after a few years of power, by poison, by the knife, or by the traditional bowstring.

Yamina realised that Mihri wanted to impress her with how much she had and how fortunate she was in her new position.

She showed her through the lattice-work of a balcony the great Central Hall of the Palace, surrounded by a dome with massive gold columns.

The windows were framed in Renaissance garlands and festoons. There were frescoed walls, all very white, fresh, and gaudy, and banal after the age-long history that had made the Seraglio so impressive.

Everywhere in the Palace there was a profusion of coloured glass, huge standards to hold the lights in glaring red, green, and blue, vases, ornaments, and even coffee-tables decorated with it.

The Sultan obviously had a decided preference for the glitter of enormous mirrors and Bohemian glass chandeliers in every colour, for glaringly painted ceilings and large and ponderous European-type chairs.

Some of the mosaics, however, were exquisite, and the carved marble with its intricate patterns had a beauty that was indescribable.

What fascinated Yamina was the fantastic extravagance which seemed outrageous when she remembered the poverty of the average Turk whom she had seen in the Bazaar and in the poorer parts of the City.

Dust-pans of solid silver struck her as unnecessary, and so were the real diamond buttons sewed onto modern kid-boots that had been imported from Paris to titillate the Harem's craving for Western chic.

There were umbrellas with gold ribs studded in sapphires, coffee-cups chunked from a single emerald, and hand-towels stiff with gold embroidery.

Coverlets of cloth-of-gold lined with sable were flung among the cushions, curtains were roped back with swags of pearls.

No favourite ever appeared before the Sultan in the same dress twice, and whatever extravagances the more-favoured women perpetrated, the bills for their finery were never questioned.

Yamina was interested in the luxury of marble-walled *toilettes,* with fountains of running water attached to every suite of rooms.

The Sultan, she was told, had a bath of solid jasper, the pipes were of gold and silver, the walls scented with roses, musk, and amber, and aloes were kept constantly burning in censers.

Yet after a very short while her interest in all these novel sights began to pall, and Yamina felt that the walls were beginning to close in on her so that she felt constricted and almost unable to breathe.

"How can I ever escape from here?" she asked Mihri when she felt it was safe to talk intimately, which was only occasionally.

Mihri shrugged her shoulders.

"I do not know," she answered. "I learnt from Sahin that there was danger of your being arrested as a spy."

"There was; they were talking of making a house-to-house search," Yamina said, "and I was afraid not only for myself, but also for Hamid."

She did not relate to Mihri what she had seen happening in the Bazaar. She felt she could not bear to speak of it.

But soon she found that almost every moment of every hour of every day she was wondering how soon she could get away and beginning to feel that it was more and more impossible.

She could not help the feeling that in every shadow there were the watchers and those who were watched.

The deaf mutes frightened her. They seemed somehow uncanny as they scuttled down the passages in their ill-fitting slippers.

There were dwarfs who capered in front of the Sultan to amuse him while the Harem could watch from behind lattice-balconies, but they seemed to Yamina to be singularly unamusing.

But always there was someone moving surreptitiously about the Palace.

Everybody walked softly on bare feet or in jewelled slippers, and there was something hushed and stealthy about it, something which made Yamina, when she was alone, shiver with fear.

Even Mihri, she felt at times, was on edge.

There were unknown, hidden, unimagined dangers in this Palace of intrigue.

Who was to know that a sherbet made of sugar and violets did not contain poison, that a jewelled dagger, richly ornamented, would not strike home as one moved down a narrow corridor?

A sip of coffee might be a sip of death, and the flutter of a rival's gauze handkerchief might conceal a death-dealing plial.

One man and so many women. One favourite and so many jealous, envious eyes, so many hearts consumed by hatred.

One evening when Mihri was showing Yamina her jewellery for the hundredth time, the diamonds, rubies, and emeralds were flashing in the sunshine coming through the windows, she said in a low voice:

"We have to make plans for you to leave!"

Yamina was suddenly alert.

"Why?"

"Because," Mihri answered, "it will not be safe for you to stay here very much longer."

"Why? Why?" Yamina enquired.

For a moment she wondered if she had in some way offended the Sultan.

She had never seen him, but she had learnt only too well that he had only to utter the fatal phrase: "Let her disappear!" for any inmate of the Harem's doom to be sealed.

She had been told with relish by one of the more elderly and embittered odalisques who had never caught the Sultan's eye that a previous Ruler in a fit of boredom had ordered his entire Harem to die overnight.

"He wished to have new faces around him!"

She was Persian and she had tried ever since Yamina had arrived to make her apprehensive and afraid.

"How were they killed?" Yamina enquired, knowing that it was expected of her.

"In the usual way," the Persian answered. "Their feet were weighted, and they were sewn into sacks and thrown into the Bosporus!"

She smiled unpleasantly as she continued:

"It is said that a diver once going beneath the waters saw them all standing upright on the bottom, bowing and swaying in the tide. Dead but still moving!"

Yamina felt herself shiver, not only at the story itself but also at the way it had been related to her.

She realised that women who had nothing to think about could allow to fester within themselves a poisonous hatred for those who were more favoured.

Now she wondered whether someone had spitefully informed the Sultan that she was not what she appeared to be, and her eyes were on Mihri questioningly as the Circassian said:

"I may be wrong, perhaps I am, but I have a feeling that His Highness Kizlar Aga is interested in you!"

"The Black Eunuch?" Yamina exclaimed. "But what do you mean? Why is he interested in me? Is he suspicious?"

"Worse than that!" Mihri replied.

She drew even closer and her lips almost touched Yamina's as she said:

"He may ask for you for his own Harem!"

"I do not understand!"

"It is conceit with the eunuchs," Mihri explained. "They are not men, but they behave as if they were. It gives them a sense of power and prestige to have women of their own, even as their Master has. The Kislar Aga has a large Harem. It is whispered that he is very cruel, that his hippopotamus-hide whip is used continually, and that his slaves are punished for the most trivial offences or for no offence at all!"

"I cannot believe it!" Yamina cried.

"It is true!" Mihri said. "And I think he wishes to own you not because you are beautiful but because he thinks you are my sister!"

"I do . . . not . . . understand," Yamina faltered again.

"He thinks I am gaining too much power over his Master," Mihri answered. "The Black Eunuchs are always afraid that the women will have more power than they have themselves. So to have a hold over me he is contriving to take you into his Harem!"

The whole idea was so horrifying that Yamina wanted to cry out, to scream. Yet she knew she must hold on tightly to her self-control, that she must not show her fear to Mihri or to anyone else.

"I will think what to do," Mihri said. "He will delay and prevaricate for a long time before he asks for you, but it is always wise in this place to be prepared. To be taken by surprise can be fatal!"

"I can see that!" Yamina exclaimed.

Despite every resolution, she glanced nervously over her shoulder, almost as if she expected to see the Black Eunuch standing behind her.

What she had now heard made her feel, as she had before she entered the Palace, that the Black Eunuchs were everything that was horrible and unclean.

She had learnt since she had been at the Dolmabahce Palace that some of the odalisques in their frustration, convinced that they would never catch the eye of the Sultan, contrived to establish a sort of relationship with the eunuchs. But the women for the most part were too frightened, especially of the Kizlar Aga himself.

"They are a resentful lot!" the Persian, who had more intelligence than most of the other women, said to Yamina. "Full of malice and envy, they lash out with their hippopotamus-hide whips!"

Some of the women took a delight in tormenting them, and they were known ironically amongst themselves as "Keeper of the Rose," or "Guardian of Delights."

If a eunuch heard them speak in such a manner their revenge was often swift and painful.

The women were never marked on their faces in case it should be noticed by the Sultan. But on other parts of the body there were scars and weals, and after such treatment the odalisque was usually disciplined into a timidity which prevented her from being anything but subservient in future.

"What makes you think that he has such an idea where I am concerned?" Yamina asked.

"Already he is beginning to tell the Sultan that it is a mistake to have my sister in the Harem, that an *Ikbal's* affection should be concentrated solely on her Master."

Mihri gave an exasperated little sound.

"I know his methods only too well! I have seen him, since I have been here, deliberately break up an affection between two women just for the joy of making them unhappy! I am told he can be very cruel to those who have been allowed to keep their children, sometimes separating a mother from her child just so that he can show his power!"

"What can we do?" Yamina asked, and her voice was hardly above a whisper.

"I shall think of something," Mihri said.

But her tone was not very convincing and Yamina thought despairingly:

'If the worst comes to the worst there is . . . always the . . . Bosporus!'

Chapter 4

Lord Castleford walked into the study where the Ambassador was sitting with his desk piled high with papers.

He looked up and when he saw who was there he gave Lord Castleford a smile which was thought in diplomatic circles to charm a bird off a tree.

"It has come!" Lord Castleford said, and there was a note of excitement in his voice.

"From Lord Palmerston?"

"Yes. His letter asks me to proceed to Athens but he says quite clearly it is only a temporary appointment."

"He has promised he will give you Paris," Lord Stratford said, "but you may have to wait a year or two. Even then you will be the youngest Ambassador in Europe."

The British Embassy in Paris was the Mecca of all aspiring Diplomats, and that Lord Castleford should be considered for such a position was almost unique in the annals of diplomatic history.

But he had proved himself so outstandingly successful in all the posts to which he had so far been appointed, and also in the role of a roving Diplomat, that Lord Stratford had been sure that he would not have gone unnoticed by the Foreign Office.

He had however made certain on his last journey to England that Lord Palmerston was aware of the many coups that Lord Castleford had brought off.

The Great Elchi could not help feeling a tremendous satisfaction that his pupil in following his own methods in dealing with foreign powers was in many ways a replica of himself when young.

Lord Castleford put the letter from the Prime Minister down on the Ambassador's desk, and Lord Stratford read it carefully before he said:

"Greece is going to be difficult, you know that!"

"You have always told me that she is the *enfant terrible* of Europe," Lord Castleford replied, "but as you were instrumental in creating the Kingdom of the Hellenes, you are responsible."

"It is not a child whose antics last year I can commend," Lord Stratford said. "And certainly not the behaviour of her King."

"I imagine His Majesty has been a disappointment," Lord Castleford remarked.

"We can only deprecate the manner in which he is supporting Russia against the Allied Powers," the Ambassador replied.

"It was to be expected," Lord Castleford murmured to himself. "The Greeks and Russians are co-Religionists, and of course Greece had been under the brutal domination of Turkey for three hundred years until Independence in 1829, and the Queen, although she is a daughter of the Grand Duke of Oldenburg, has Russian blood in her veins."

"That does not excuse King Otho for choosing the moment when we had a war on our hands to make a bid for popular support in an attempt to enlarge Greece's territory!"

Lord Stratford's voice sharpened as he went on: "Until now there has been no major breach of the peace between Greece and Turkey for twenty-five years, with the exception of certain frontier incidents in 1847."

"Then last year, while they invaded Epirus and were defeated by the Turks at Péta," Lord Castleford said reflectively, "they had no success in Thessaly."

"Nevertheless, we were right in landing British and French troops at Piraeus to enforce Greek neutrality," Lord Stratford said, "and we shall keep a force there so that Greece's frontiers will remain unchanged."

"I understand the people applauded their King's aggressive attitude," Lord Castleford said with a slight touch of sarcasm in his voice.

"They only applaud him when he is trying to make fresh conquests. At home he is considered a tyrant and the country has seething pockets of resentment which sooner or later will end in revolution," Lord Stratford prophesied.

"That is something I must obviously try to prevent," Lord Castleford remarked, "at least until the War is at an end."

"The War!" Lord Stratford gave a little sigh.

"How is it progressing?" Lord Castleford enquired. "Have you any definite news of the siege?"

"I am convinced, and I shall be greatly surprised if I am not right," Lord Stratford replied, "that Sebastopol will fall at the end of the Summer or in the early Autumn. Meantime, soldiers are still being killed in action and although the Hospital arrangements are now better than they were before, we are still losing a large number of men from dysentery and from incompetent medical treatment."

"I am sure Miss Nightingale will not agree with you there," Lord Castleford said with a smile.

"Miss Nightingale has performed miracles!" Lord Stratford answered. "But she cannot in a few months overcome the prejudices and the jealousy of the Doctors who often deliberately try to obstruct her work."

"I am wondering why you think Sebastopol will ever fall," Lord Castleford questioned, following his own train of thought. "Despite the continual bombardment, I am beginning to think that the Russians are right and it is impregnable."

"It will fall eventually!" Lord Stratford asserted without further explanation. "But as usual, Napoleon III is interfering and hampering the Turkish troops, who fight magnificently if they are left alone."

Lord Castleford gave a little smile at the note of warmth in the Ambassador's voice.

His partiality and love for the Turks was known to everyone. He alone was responsible for the reform of the Ottoman Empire and the admiration it had evoked in Europe was entirely due to his efforts.

But now the Great Elchi forgot his Turkish friends in his desire to help Lord Castleford in what would undoubtedly be one of the most difficult diplomatic posts to which he had ever been appointed.

"King Otho lacks the qualities of mind and character which are essential to his position," he said slowly. "I said to him once: 'The throne of Greece has not been set up as an idle pageant.'"

"Did he resent your speaking to him like that?" Lord Castleford asked.

"I do not think so," the Ambassador replied. "And anyway, he could not afford to quarrel with me. The Greeks themselves gave me a most tumultuous welcome, and a King, however much he may sympathise with Russia, is frightened of offending England."

"I have always heard that His Majesty is an attractive man," Lord Castleford said.

"Certainly where the fair sex is concerned," Lord Stratford agreed. "When he was first made King of the Hellenes he had all the good looks and the charm of the Bavarians. But he also had their propensity for running after women and for women running after them!"

"I have heard there have been a number of love-affairs," Lord Castleford said, "including one with the notorious Lady Ellenborough."

Lord Stratford laughed.

"The least said about that the better! Lady Ellenborough set the whole of Athens by its ears after she not only took the King as a lover, but also, having married His Majesty's Aide-de-Camp, she then fancied an Albanian General who swooped down on Athens from his mountain lair and was soon the most talked-of person in Court!"

"I have also heard, although it may be untrue," Lord Castleford said, "that Queen Amelie herself had a tender regard for General Hadji-Petros."

"I believe that was true," Lord Stratford replied, "but she did not stand a chance against Jane Ellenborough, who with her fair hair and blue eyes had an attraction for men which made her irresistible."

He glanced at Lord Castleford and thought he was looking cynical.

"There are women like that," he said, "but not perhaps so commonly in England as in other parts of the world. Jane Ellenborough, whom I knew when she was quite young, was tempestuous, impulsive, incurably romantic, and extremely promiscuous. Yet men who were no less sophisticated and cynical than you, Vernon, fell head-over-heels in love with her!"

"You frighten me!" Lord Castleford said. "I am glad that Lady Ellenborough is now too old for me to need to avoid her, but she sounds even in her heyday the type of woman in whom I would have no interest."

Lord Stratford sat back in his chair and there was a twinkle in his eyes as he said:

"You are very confident of yourself, Vernon. It is strange that in all your travels around the world I have never heard of any scandal or even gossip connected with your name."

"As you know, My Lord, I am wedded to my career!" Lord Castleford replied. "While I find some women amusing, I would never permit one to interfere with my ambitions or my plans for my future."

"You have never been in love?" Lord Stratford enquired.

"Never, if by that you mean a maudlin state in which a man can no longer think clearly, when he believes the world is well lost for the sensations evoked in him which can be nothing but transient."

There was silence for a moment. Then the Ambassador said:

"This is an aspect of your character, Vernon, that I have never considered before. I have the feeling that you are missing something—something which is important to your development as a man."

Lord Castleford laughed.

"You talk almost as if I were peculiar in some way," he said. "I assure you I find women an entrancing pastime, and I will admit to having at various times in my life found certain of the fair sex quite irresistible!"

He gave Lord Stratford an amused glance as he said:

"But I must disappoint you, My Lord, and say that never for one moment has there been a woman who could have deflected me from my chosen path! Quite frankly, if I am honest, there has never been a woman who, if it came to a choice between her and my work, has not been easily dispensable."

"Perhaps one day . . ." Lord Stratford began tentatively.

Lord Castleford interrupted him.

"I know what you are going to say, but the answer is no! Some men are self-sufficient in themselves and I am one of them. A woman is a play-thing."

He paused to say almost provocatively:

"In my opinion, the Sultan has entirely the right idea. He keeps his toys locked up in a cupboard where only he can take them out to play with them and where he need not even think about them when he has other, more important matters on his mind."

"That is an Oriental outlook," Lord Stratford remarked.

"Which has much to commend it," Lord Castleford answered. "Think how much easier our task would be if there were no Lady Ellenboroughs taking a Royal lover or upsetting a country by running away with an Albanian General."

He paused to go on:

"Do you not imagine that diplomacy in Paris would be far less complicated if Napoleon III were not obsessed by his mistresses? Their number is legion, and each one makes him less effective as an Emperor and more vulnerable to public resentment."

He looked at the Ambassador for a moment before he said:

"You do not agree with me?"

"I was just wondering," Lord Stratford replied, "whether you are at heart a puritan or a prude."

"I am neither!" Lord Castleford replied. "I am an extremely practical man who sees his duty to his country as a straight, clear road ahead of him. I have no wish to linger amongst the flowers by the roadside. If I occasionally stop to pick one, I know it will fade quickly and will not become an encumbrance to delay my progress unduly."

He smiled at the look on the Ambassador's face as he went on:

"Women are the flowers of life. Once one has picked them, one expects nothing but that they should fade and eventually die."

"It is extraordinary!" Lord Stratford said. "I can say quite honestly, Vernon, that you shock me. I did not expect to find in you, my most brilliant and favoured pupil, a man so cynical, one who appears to have an almost jaded view of life."

"I promise you I am not jaded!" Lord Castleford replied. "Cynical, perhaps; practical, yes; and strictly unromantic!"

"The Athenian women are very beautiful!" Lord Stratford said softly.

"I shall look on them with pleasure!" Lord Castleford replied.

"And Paris, you will find, is filled with the most deliberately alluring women the world has ever known."

"There I agree with you," Lord Castleford said, "but in Paris there is no pretence. The alluring women to whom you refer so warmly all have their price. It is just a question of whom you can afford, and the price being paid, it is entirely a question of sensual enjoyment without any aftermath of reproach, recrimination, or, far worse, tears!"

Lord Stratford looked amused.

He could understand now why Lord Castleford, who was extremely good-looking, could speak so scathingly of women.

Obviously he had been pursued relentlessly and perhaps even persecuted by women who to him had meant a brief, transitory liaison, but which they wished to prolong into something far more serious and permanent.

Lord Stratford could remember the same sort of thing happening to him in his youth when he had been as good-looking as Lord Castleford.

Even now, he thought, there were times when a woman looked at him with an expression in her eyes that he could not misunderstand, and when it was difficult to extract himself from an embarrassing situation, especially if his wife was not with him.

At the same time, he could not help thinking that Lord Castleford was too self-confident, and that it would in fact do him good if he fell in love and suffered the heart-burn, the pangs of despair, and the agony of indecision which most men passed through at some time in their lives.

But he was too experienced a Diplomat to say anything. He merely changed the subject to talk of Greece, in which Lord Castleford was at once absorbedly interested.

The following day when Lord Castleford returned from riding, which was an exercise he preferred above all others, Lord Stratford had news for him.

"I have discovered that the *Himalaya* will be leaving here the day after tomorrow," he said, "carrying a large number of casualties who are too badly wounded to return to the Front, but well enough to endure the journey home."

"The ship will take me to Athens?" Lord Castleford enquired.

"That is what I have arranged," Lord Stratford replied, "and let me say that you are lucky the *Himalaya* is available."

"I have heard of her."

"It was not until the beginning of this year," the Ambassador went on, "that the Government realised how foolish their policy was of sending out Cavalry and artillery in sailing-vessels.

"It rendered many of the horses unfit for service and the Military Commanders warned the Government very strongly of the hardship that was endured by the Cavalry Regiments."

"You would think they would have understood it from the very first!" Lord Castleford said, "and moved more quickly."

"Do Governments ever act swiftly?" Lord Stratford asked bitterly. "The only time they expect miracles is from people like myself! I still smile when I remember that the Duke of Newcastle asked me for thirty thousand pairs of Wellington boots, imagining I could find them overnight in the Bazaar!"

Lord Castleford laughed.

"Did His Grace really think that?"

"He did indeed," Lord Stratford replied, "and was quite surprised when I found it a difficult task!"

"The stupidity of the Army appals me!"

"I agree with you, but it is something we must not say in public," Lord Stratford replied.

"No, indeed! But you were telling me about the ship."

"Yes, of course. At the beginning of this year the Government bought two of the fastest P & O steamships which had actually proved too expensive for the company to run. The *Himalaya,* 3,438 tons, is the largest and fastest ship afloat."

"It is a screw-steamer, I believe."

"It is," Lord Stratford agreed, "and she completed the journey from England to here in eleven days, nineteen hours, while the *Thirteenth Light Dragoons* spent almost eight weeks on the voyage by sail!"

"So I shall travel to Greece in luxury!" Lord Castleford smiled.

"I have made arrangements for the best cabin on board to be put at your disposal. As the ship is overcrowded, it is doubtful if you can be allotted a Suite, but I am sure that my note to the Captain will effect all that is possible."

"Thank you," Lord Castleford said. "It is pleasant to think that I shall not arrive in Athens exhausted and perhaps bruised from a rough passage in a sailing-ship."

"Before you go," Lord Stratford interposed, "I consider it to be of the utmost importance for you to meet the Sultan."

He paused before continuing:

"I intended to arrange a meeting while you were here, but I did not realise it was a matter of such urgency. It is, as you know, important that you should keep the peace between these two countries, and the fact that the Turks expelled all Greek citizens from Smyrna and Constantinople last year will not make relations any easier."

"It was the fault of the Greeks. They started the fighting!" Lord Castleford said.

"The Greeks never accept that anything is their fault," the Ambassador replied, "and although the King is Bavarian, that is one characteristic he has filched from his adopted country."

"You are making me nervous!"

Lord Castleford spoke in a voice that showed he was not serious.

"You will manage this post as you have done all your others," Lord Stratford assured him, "with intelligence, firmness, and a diplomacy which has already ingratiated you with the Ministry of Foreign Affairs."

"I hope you are right!"

But there was no doubt from Lord Castleford's tone that he was supremely self-confident.

Lord Stratford gave a little sigh as if he was half-disappointed over something he could not put into words. Then he picked up his pen.

"I will write and request an audience for you with the Sultan," he said. "I know he will want to meet you and to know him personally will, I am sure, assist you in your relations with King Otho."

* * *

Yamina found it difficult to sleep in the Harem. She lay awake worrying over what Mihri had told her about the intentions of the Black Eunuch.

She could hardly believe they were true, and yet she knew Mihri would not frighten her unnecessarily. She could not help, now that she was looking out for it, noticing that the Kizlar Aga's eyes often rested on her when he entered the Harem.

She tried to efface herself, to make herself unobtrusive, and yet she had the feeling that it was impossible to hide: whatever she did, however she behaved, she was seen and watched.

Mihri, she knew, was trying desperately hard to find out what was afoot so that they would not be taken by surprise.

Yamina did not know whether it was significant or merely routine when she was ordered by the *Haremlik*—the Lady Stewardess—to attend a first lesson in the art of love.

Since her arrival she had been accepted as Mihri's sister, and therefore in the eyes of the Harem was not the ordinary odalisque who had been brought in for the Sultan's pleasure.

But every new-comer was forced to take part in the teaching, which was given by the older and more experienced women and supervised by the *Sultan Valideh* herself.

It would be impossible for Yamina to be treated differently and not to be subject to the usual rules.

She therefore told Mihri what her orders were, but the *Ikbal* held up her hands in horror.

"No! No! This must not happen!" she cried.

"Buy why?" Yamina asked.

"Because you will be shocked!"

"Shocked?" Yamina questioned in surprise.

"The Eastern idea of love-making is very different from yours as a Russian or mine as a Circassian."

Yamina looked at her wide-eyed and Mihri went on:

"At first I could not believe what I was hearing, but then I told myself that if I was to have any power in the Harem, if I was ever to rise from an odalisque to a *Kadin*, then I must learn everything the others learnt and do it better!"

"I understand," Yamina said.

"For me there is no escape," Mihri said, "I am here, this is my life; and now I am grateful, very grateful, that I listened to what I was taught. I realise it was important from the point of view of a Turk."

She paused to say almost violently:

"But you, Mistress, are different."

Yamina started and put her fingers to her lips.

"Be careful!" she whispered. "I am your sister."

"You are someone I have respected and honoured since first I came to you in Balaclava," Mihri said.

Now her voice was so low it was hard to hear the words.

"One day," she went on, "you will marry a man of your own blood. Then it would be wrong, very wrong, for you to know the tricks, the wiles, the enticements that the Orientals expect as a matter of course from their women."

"Would it really matter?" Yamina asked.

"I know that a Circassian would think it wrong and perhaps disgusting," Mihri said, "and to a Russian it would be the same."

"But I must do as I am told," Yamina protested.

"Perhaps eventually there will be no escape," Mihri replied, "but at the moment we can play for time. When your lesson is due you will be ill. If you do not think you can pretend well enough to deceive the *Haremlik*, then I will give you a little opium, enough to make you sleepy."

"No, no, I am sure I can pretend," Yamina said, "but eventually it will be impossible for them not to realise I am playing truant."

"We cannot think too far ahead," Mihri answered. "Tonight when I am with the Sultan I will find out to whom he is granting audience. I have an idea of how I can help you to escape, but at the moment it is very vague."

"Tell me," Yamina pleaded, but Mihri shook her head.

"It is always unlucky to talk of a wish until you know it can be fulfilled."

Yamina smiled. Everyone in the Harem was extremely superstitious.

What the women enjoyed more than anything else was having their fortunes told. Occasionally a fortune-teller would be smuggled in with the contrivance of the Black Eunuchs, who would expect to be paid for their trouble in jewels and other valuables.

Even the enticement of diamonds paled beside the thrill brought by the fortune-teller, reading the lines of their hands or shuffling the cards.

For an odalisque to be told that sooner or later she would catch the eye of the Sultan and that she would become a *Kadin* was to keep her happy for weeks. Only time could dim the glow of hope that such prophecies engendered.

The women were always relating stories of prophecies that came true.

The beautiful Aimée Dubacq de Rivery was told by an old witch in Martinique that the ship on which she travelled to France would be seized by Corsairs and she would be captured and placed in a Seraglio.

"There," the old woman went on, "you will give birth to a son, who will reign gloriously, but the steps of his throne will be dyed with the blood of his predecessor."

It had all come true.

Because Aimée was so beautiful, the Algerian Corsairs reserved her for Baba Mohammed Ben Osman of Algiers. He realised the moment he saw her that she would be a worthy offering to the Sultan himself.

The odalisques told with pleasure and excitement how Aimée had reached Constantinople and, on being received by the Chief Eunuch at the Gate of Felicity, had fainted away.

At first she had fought against everyone in the Harem and the fate that awaited her.

Then when she had talked with the Kizler Aga, who at that time was a moderate and humane man, her thrifty French mind had realised what a splendid fate might await her.

Obediently she passed through the "*Académie d'Amour*" and become perfect in every seductive art her Royal Master's jaded appetites might demand.

Everyone wanted to tell Yamina the end of the story.

When Aimée Dubacq de Rivery was escorted to the Sultan, she found he was not "a terrible Turk" but a cultivated voluptuary.

To him Aimée seemed a creature apart; her blonde beauty and her Western intellect delighted him.

Very soon the old witch's prophecy began to come true.

Aimée was known as "*Naksh*, the Beautiful One," and was firmly installed as the Sultan's favourite.

When her son, Mahmoud, was born, Aimée found herself the key figure in the succession to the Ottoman throne. When the old Sultan died, his nephew became Sultan Salim III and relied on Aimée's support behind the scenes.

He developed an enthusiasm for everything that was French and Aimée's power was almost unsurpassed.

But the intrigue and violence in the Seraglio was only waiting.

Sultan Salim died fighting against those who would destroy him together with Mahmoud, Aimée's child.

But his death led the way for Mahmoud to become Sultan and once again Aimée was in power.

For years she fought for him, directed him, guided him, and became in the process one of the most powerful women the Ottoman Empire had ever known.

As *Sultan Valideh* she reigned supreme and it was always said that the reason Napoleon Bonaparte got no-where when he wooed the Sultan was that Aimée hated him.

She was the cousin of the wife he had divorced, the Empress Josephine, and they had been companions in Martinique.

For thirty-three years the little French girl from Martinique knew great triumphs and glories.

When she was dying in 1817 a Priest was called to the Convent of St. Antoine in Pera. There he administered the Last Sacraments to an unknown woman and as she died he gave her absolution.

The sole witness of the scene, a bearded man, flung himself down beside the bed, weeping.

It was the "Successor of the Prophet," the "Master of Masters," "the Sultan Giaour," crying out to Allah for the loss of his beloved mother.

Such tales helped pass the long hours in the Harem just as the setting out of the cards or the staring into a crystal ball brought a little ray of hope that fate would be kind and the Sultan's eye would turn from Mihri to one of his other women.

But Yamina found herself watching the Black Eunuch, listening to the whispers of the slaves and wondering if someone was plotting against her, against Mihri, against the Sultan himself!

Fear was always there like the hiss of a snake in the grass, sometimes so faint as to make her think she had imagined it, at other times so real and poisonous that it was impossible not to tremble.

"What shall I do?" Yamina asked over and over again.

At night she would try to pray, but somehow the God who had been with her all her life seemed lost beside the importance of Allah, to whom every good Moslem prayed twice a day.

Life went on, the unhurried, organised, traditional life of the Harem, where everyone had their allotted place: the Reader of the Koran, the Head-Nurse, the Keeper of the Baths, and even the copper-boilers for the *hammen*, the gardeners, the carpenters, the plasterers, and the *Tressed Halberdiers*, or corps of manual workers, wood-cutters, and body-guards who came into the Harem, but under the strictest rules.

The name of *Tressed Halberdiers* was derived from two long locks of artificial hair which fell on each side of their faces.

These were originally worn to prevent them from casting any side-long glances on those whom they should not see.

But there was in fact never anyone about when they appeared; for the warning cry of: "*Helvet! Helvet!*" ensured that the Black Eunuchs took care that their charges were invisible and under lock and key.

On Mihri's insistence Yamina managed to avoid going for her lessons in love.

First there was the excuse that she was ill, the next day it was possible to say that Mihri required her, although, as the Circassian pointed out, this was an excuse they could only use once.

On the third day, just as Yamina was wondering what she could say to the *Haremlik*, she was called to Mihri's room.

She saw at once that the *Ikbal* was looking excited, and at the same time extremely beautiful.

Her clothes were more splendid than usual and she

had diamonds round her neck and on her wrists that Yamina had not seen before.

"What is it?" she asked as soon as the door closed and they were alone.

Mihri put her fingers to her lips. Then taking Yamina by the hand she drew her across the room to the window. Here it was impossible for an eavesdropper to listen inside a hollow wall, as could happen in the other rooms of the Palace.

Putting her arms round Yamina, she embraced her, whispering as she did so:

"I have a plan for you to leave, but we have not much time!"

"What is it?" Yamina asked, aware that her heart had begun to beat quickly at the thought of escape.

"First you must change your clothes," Mihri said.

"But why?" Yamina asked.

"Leave everything to me," Mihri said, hardly breathing.

She moved from Yamina's side and clapped her hands loudly.

When the slaves came running at the summons she cried out in a voice of fury:

"Is this the way you carry out my orders? Are these the shabby garments you give my sister? She has worn that dress two—no, three times! You insult me—I—the *Ikbal*, the favoured of the Padishah!"

The slaves were thrown into consternation.

"No, no, Mistress! We did not mean any harm. The odalisque chose her own garments. We are not responsible for them!"

"Of course you are responsible for them!" Mihri stormed. "I am ashamed, utterly ashamed that my sister should be humiliated by your inefficiency, your incompetence! She must change immediately! Bring in the trunk you will find in the passage which contains new garments I have ordered for myself, but in which I will now dress my sister."

Terrified at their Mistress's anger, the slaves ran to obey.

They came back carrying an ornate trunk painted in the manner that found favour in Eastern eyes and fastened with gold locks and hinges.

With trembling fingers they unfastened the *entari* which Yamina had thought when she put it on was extremely attractive. But now from the trunk they took out clothes that were far more luxurious—in fact, equalled only by those worn by Mihri herself.

Half-a-dozen hands robed Yamina in a gauze chemise, so fine it would have passed through a gold ring. It was open to the waist, revealing her breasts.

Vast *chalvari* were fastened at her ankles with jewelled bands, and a crimson silk *entari* embroidered with precious stones was fastened with pearl buttons. The sleeves trailed almost to the floor, and the girdle was of pearls and amethysts which also decorated the stomacher-clasp.

A molten shower of diamonds glittered in the gold chains to be threaded through her dark hair, and there were rings for her fingers and bracelets for her wrists.

"That is better!" Mihri said, who had stood watching the women at work, a scowl between her eyes.

"You may go!" she went on. "But never allow my sister to appear again in such a manner or I will have you whipped until you scream for mercy!"

The slaves rushed trembling from the room.

When they had gone Mihri stood for a moment as if to make certain that no-one was listening at the door. Then she said to Yamina in a whisper:

"Get into the trunk!"

Yamina looked at her in astonishment.

"What do you . . . mean?" she asked.

"What I say! It is the only way you can escape. The Sultan told me last night that he was receiving guests this morning. Because he does not wish to see them until late, since he wishes to be with me first, he is sending one of them, I did not hear his name, in the Royal Caique to a ship that is anchored out in the Bosporus."

"And you mean . . . that I shall . . . go with him . . . in the trunk?" Yamina asked.

"It is the only way," Mihri said. "But the ship is English!"

Yamina looked at her wide-eyed.

The word "English" sounded ominous in her ears. At the same time, she knew that even to be a prisoner of the English was at this moment preferable to being taken to the Harem of the Black Eunuch.

She had not wasted her time these last few days since Mihri had told her what was intended.

There had been odalisques who were only too willing to tell her stories of what happened in the Black Eunuch's household.

Of screams that were heard in the darkness of the night, of women who disappeared after it was known that the Kizlar Aga was angry with them, of beatings, torture, and cruelties which were so unpleasant that Yamina tried not to listen to the details of them.

It all added up to a horrifying picture which had made her even more terrified than she was already!

She knew with a desperation born of despair that if eventually the Black Eunuch asked for her and persuaded the Sultan to give her to him as a present, then she must kill herself.

It would not be difficult, there were innumerable ways available in the Harem of taking one's own life; but something young and resilient within her rebelled at the thought of dying.

She wanted to live!

There was so much she wanted to do, so much she wanted to learn, so much she wanted to feel.

Always in the past there had seemed an endless future ahead, years of living, so that there was no need to hurry through the present; but now she had begun to count every minute as if it were her last.

The sunshine through the windows made her long for a freedom that she felt would never be hers again.

She would think of herself galloping round the Estate at Balaclava on one of the fine horses that her father had provided for her.

She would even think to herself of the horse on which she had last ridden, sitting in front of Lord Castleford.

His arm had been strong and protective, and although he was a stranger whom she had never seen before, she had known that she was safe with him.

Not only had he carried her away from the horror and the dangers of the Bazaar, but also there was something about his self-confidence and his faith in himself that, while she resented it, gave her a sense of comfort.

She found herself wondering what he would have done if she had called to him when she was being carried away to the Palace, from the burning house which had contained her father's body.

She could imagine his astonishment if she had pulled back the curtains and told the deaf mutes to set down their burden.

They would not have heard her, but Hamid would have made a sign to them which they would have obeyed.

She could imagine herself stepping from the Sedan chair and going to the side of Lord Castleford's horse.

She would have looked up at him as he sat there, so imposing, so distinguished! And yet, even though he was English, he was a man whom she could trust because he was a gentleman.

"Save me! Save me!"

She could hear herself saying the words—and yet she had not said them!

She had let herself be carried away to the Harem, but never had she anticipated anything so terrifying as what awaited her at this moment.

She could understand the Black Eunuch's motive for wanting her. She could understand his jealousy of Mihri.

At the same time, the odalisques told her that he had favourites among his slaves, women he caressed, women who in some way that was difficult to understand attracted him, even though he was not a man.

Yamina felt herself shudder with an inexpressible disgust and she knew that anything was preferable to remaining in the Harem and have that horror hanging over her head.

But still she hesitated.

"You are quite sure if I do this it will not hurt you . . . you will not be punished for my disappearance?" she asked Mihri.

"I have thought of that," Mihri answered. "Your shoes will be found later tonight beside the water. Sahin will report that he saw a figure in the garden, but when he reached the edge of the sea it was too late."

"Sahin is helping you in this?" Yamina asked unnecessarily.

She knew that the two Circassians, both coming from her home at Balaclava, would contrive together to help her.

It was extraordinary, she thought, that they had never forgotten the happiness they had known there and that to serve her they should be prepared to risk their own lives.

She put her arms round Mihri and kissed her on both cheeks.

"I have no words in which to thank you," she said. "I can only say that if I reach safety my thoughts will always be with you. My love is yours already!"

She saw the quick tears come into Mihri's beautiful blue eyes. Then the Circassian bent her head and kissed both her hands.

"God be with you, Mistress," she said, "and keep you safe."

Then as if she realised that time was passing she almost pushed Yamina into the painted trunk.

The soft sable of a fur-lined caftan lined the bottom of it, and as Yamina crouched down Mihri started to heap the garments on top of her, until she was covered with the soft silks, satins, and gauzes. Then the *Ikbal* slammed the trunk to and clapped her hands.

When once again the slaves came running she was standing at the door of the *toilette* and was speaking to Yamina as if she were inside.

"You must have jewellery," she remarked.

Then to the slaves she said:

"Take the trunk back to Sahin. He has my instructions to bring new clothes from the Bazaar. Not even these are worthy of my sister! And if it is not done immediately, I shall complain to the Sultan, and you will all be punished for your negligence!"

Hastily the slaves fastened the locks of the trunk and Yamina, crouching down inside, heard slow footsteps approaching and knew that they had summoned the deaf mutes.

It was they who did all the carrying in the Harem, and as they lifted up the trunk Yamina wondered if they would query the fact that it was so heavy.

Then she remembered that they could not speak even as they could not hear; nevertheless, they had a kind of sign-language of their own by which they could communicate with one another.

But apparently they were not suspicious, and Yamina found herself being carried across the room and through the door, while Mihri's voice ranted and raved at the slaves in a manner which was bound to distract their attention.

It was dark inside the trunk, but Yamina soon realised that on each side there were small holes which had been punctured to let in the air, but which also let in the light.

Without moving she could put her eye to one of them and see that they were proceeding down the narrow corridors and the back stairs which led to the side of the Palace.

As they reached the ground floor, she was aware by the robes she could see through her peep-hole that someone else had joined them.

It took her a moment or two to realise who it was, until with a leap of her heart she knew it was Sahin!

She thought that the deaf mutes would go outside, but instead he was leading them right across the Palace through narrow corridors, until after walking for a long time there was bright light and Yamina knew they were now outside in the garden.

The sun was percolating through her air-holes, golden and warm, and now suddenly something glimmered almost blindingly and she knew it was the Bosporus.

There was the noise of men talking, the trunk was lifted from the hands of the deaf mutes, and as Yamina saw the glimmer of a gilt colonnette she knew that she was on the Royal Caique.

She was set down suddenly with a bang that made her gasp with the shock of it, and now there was the distinct sensation of a boat rising and falling on the water and the murmur of the rowers as they waited with their gold-tipped oars.

Yamina, feeling a little cramped, moved very cautiously into a more comfortable position.

The silk clothes that Mihri had piled on top of her felt heavy, but she dared to push them only a little aside in case someone should open the trunk.

It was most unlikely, but still it would be crazy to take risks at this moment.

She could not help being aware that if she was discovered and taken back into the Harem, not only would she be severely punished but Mihri also would be involved and probably lose the favour of the Sultan.

Sahin, too, would certainly lose his life for assisting a woman to escape.

"Please, God, do not let me be discovered!" Yamina prayed.

Perhaps it was her imagination but she felt already, because she was not overshadowed in a building in which everyone prayed incessantly to Allah, that her prayers seemed more fervent and she could hope that they were being heard.

"Help me! Please help me!" she whispered beneath her breath, and at that moment she heard English voices.

At first she could not hear what was said; she only knew by the intonation that the men approaching were speaking in English.

Then suddenly it was quite easy to hear clearly a voice saying:

"I wish you *bon voyage*, dear boy. Write to me in detail of everything you find on arrival. You know how interested I shall be."

"You know that I shall need your help," a voice replied, and Yamina drew in her breath.

There was no mistaking that cold, rather aloof tone. At the same time, the voice had a depth that was all its own.

She could hardly believe it was possible, and yet when he spoke again she knew it was Lord Castleford who had spoken.

"Thank you, My Lord, not only for my visit but also for everything you have done for me."

"Take care of yourself."

As he made no reply, Lord Castleford must have stepped aboard.

Yamina could actually hear his steps on the white wood deck. Then she heard Sahin speak.

"There is a present aboard, Your Excellency," he said in most respectful tones.

"A present?" Lord Castleford enquired.

"From the most favoured, the most honoured *Ikbal*, Your Excellency! She bids Your Lordship a safe journey, but asks that you will have the present with you in your cabin and not send it to the hold. It is of great value, Your Excellency, and its contents are also perishable."

"Will you convey my gratitude to the giver of such a present?" Lord Castleford asked. "And tell the Honourable Lady that her wishes shall be complied with."

"Your Excellency is very gracious! Here is the key."

Yamina could imagine Sahin bowing low as the

boat moved away from the white marble steps, and the oarsmen dressed in white with scarlet fezes began to ply their gold-tipped oars.

She could now hear the faint splash of the waves against the bow and the orders of the Commander of the Caique, and they were moving faster and faster over the sea.

Yamina knew that Lord Castleford would have seated himself under the dome of crimson velvet, on the silk divan on which the Sultan reclined.

It was, she was sure, unusual for him to lend his Caique to anyone except another King or Ruler, and she knew it was because he wished to honour the Great Elchi himself that his guest should be treated in such a Royal manner.

Now she could feel the sea-wind coming through the air-holes in the trunk and she drew in deep breaths of it, knowing that all the time she had been waiting at the water's edge she had been tense and constrained and held her breath.

It would have been so easy for someone to give the alarm, for someone to suspect that the painted trunk was carrying contraband of some sort to the English ship that was waiting for them.

Yamina knew exactly what the ship they were approaching would look like.

She had seen them so often moving up the Bosporus, carrying more soldiers to fight against her countrymen.

The new ships combined sail and steam and were three-masters with a short funnel amidships.

They certainly did not look as beautiful as the old sailing-ships with their high masts and intricate rigging.

But Yamina had been with her father when he had been invited aboard some of the Russian steamships in the Black Sea.

She had learnt then that the days of sail were over and that human ingenuity had brought new inventions to the nineteenth century which had made the world a smaller place than it had ever seemed before.

The Caique was still moving as swiftly as twelve men were able to pull it through the water. Then she heard a sudden sharp command, and though it was impossible for Yamina to see anything she was sure they were approaching the steamship.

There were more commands and now she could hear the throbbing of great engines somewhere in the vicinity.

A moment later she could hear the oars being first elevated, then shipped, and she guessed that ropes had been let down the side of the ship to which the crew of the Caique would cling so as to steady their boat.

There would be a rope-ladder up which Lord Castleford must climb aboard.

She heard his voice, calm and authoritative, say to the Commander of the Caique:

"Thank you for bringing me here."

He spoke in Turkish and the man replied:

"It has been an honour, Your Excellency. May we wish you a safe journey?"

"Thank you," Lord Castleford replied.

Yamina was sure that he had his foot on the bottom rung of the rope-ladder when suddenly, with a fear that felt like the thrust of a knife, she thought he must have forgotten about his present and she would be left behind.

Then as she held her breath and started to will him wildly not to forget, she heard him say:

"Be careful how that trunk is lifted aboard. It may contain something which is breakable."

"Of course, Your Excellency!"

Yamina felt herself being lifted from the deck. Ropes must have been attached to the trunk, for now she was being hauled up the side, the trunk banging occasionally against the ship as it rocked on the waves.

There was a thump as she was set down on deck.

"Welcome aboard, My Lord!" she heard an English voice say.

Then before Lord Castleford could reply the man went on:

"Your other luggage has already been taken by your Valet to your cabin, My Lord. Would you wish this trunk you have brought with you to be placed in the hold?"

There was a moment's pause, almost as if Lord Castleford was deciding what he would say.

Then he answered:

"No! Have it taken to my cabin."

"Very good, My Lord, and now if you will come this way the Captain is waiting to receive you."

Yamina realised that again she had been holding her breath, and now it escaped her lips with a hissing sound.

It did not matter, she thought, even if someone heard her! Nothing mattered! She had escaped from the Harem!

She need no longer be afraid of the Black Eunuch.

The relief made her feel faint as she whispered to herself:

"Thank you . . . God! Thank . . . you!"

Chapter 5

"I hope you will be comfortable, M'Lord."

Lord Castleford looked round the single cabin which he had been allotted.

The Captain had explained with many apologies that it had been impossible to give him two, as the ship was so crowded that every available cabin had three or four men in it.

He had given Lord Castleford instead what had been the Sitting-Room of the most expensive and luxurious Suite when the *Himalaya* had been in ordinary passenger service.

It was in fact the size of two or three cabins thrown into one, and there was in one corner a large four-poster brass bedstead of the type with which the P & O had furnished their latest steamship, the fastest and most luxurious vessel afloat.

The mosquito-net used for far-Eastern runs was swirled round the top, and supported by its four shining posts it looked rather like a galleon waiting to set its sails.

There was a thick carpet on the floor and two comfortable arm-chairs, besides a table fixed in case of rough weather, and several other pieces of furniture.

The port-holes were large and curtained and there was, the best luxury of all, a bath-room opening out of the cabin.

Lord Castleford smiled.

"I think I can manage with this," he said. "After all, it is only for one or two nights."

"I am glad it is to your satisfaction, My Lord," Jenkins replied.

There had been a slightly worried look on his thin face as he watched Lord Castleford looking round the cabin.

If his Master was made uncomfortable, Jenkins always took it as a personal insult to himself.

He had been in Lord Castleford's service for eight years and he was an excellent traveller. In fact His Lordship had said often enough that half of his success in the East was due entirely to Jenkins's care of him.

"I've arranged, M'Lord," the Valet went on now, "for you to have your meals here, and I have already spoken to the Cook, who is only too grateful for me to give him a hand in the preparation of your dishes."

He paused before he added:

"I have of course brought a considerable amount of food with me from the Embassy. His Excellency's Chef was most obliging!"

"I am sure you have thought of everything, Jenkins," Lord Castleford said in a slightly bored voice.

He enjoyed the results of Jenkins's meticulous planning, but he found it tedious to listen to long explanations as to how his successes, as they undoubtedly were, were achieved.

"Would you like anything now, M'Lord?"

"Nothing, thank you," Lord Castleford replied. "I had a light meal with His Excellency before we left the Embassy. It was early but as I was out riding at seven A.M. this morning, I was hungry enough to enjoy what I ate."

"I can believe that, M'Lord."

"You can bring me some tea at four o'clock. Until then I intend to work on my papers. You have managed to procure a desk for me, I see."

"Yes, M'Lord. I had it moved in from one of the holds where quite a large amount of furniture has been stored while the ship is carrying troops."

"Thank you, Jenkins."

"I've also managed to find a special place for Your Lordship's luggage on this deck. I don't know, however, what you wish me to do with the painted trunk you brought with you when you came aboard."

Lord Castleford looked round and saw that the trunk had been placed against one of the walls so that he had not noticed it when he entered the cabin.

"Shall I have it put with the other luggage, M'Lord?" Jenkins enquired.

"I had better first see what it contains," Lord Castleford said after a moment's pause. "The eunuch who gave me the key said it was something perishable."

He felt in his pockets and found the gold key that Sahin had given him.

"Unlock it, Jenkins. I will inspect it later."

"Very good, M'Lord."

Lord Castleford saw that there was a newspaper lying on the table in the centre of the room. He picked it up, opened it, and finding something to interest him in the centre pages sat down in an arm-chair to read it.

While he had been with the Captain the ship had started to move down the Bosporus. It was now leaving behind the domes and spires, the white-walled Mosques, kiosks, and Palaces and steaming out into the open waters of the Sea of Marmora.

Lord Castleford was however not interested. He had seen it all before and instead he concentrated on his newspaper, which, although many days old, gave him news of Europe that had not yet reached the British Embassy.

Jenkins went from the cabin, closing the door behind him, and there was only the throb of the ship's engines and the cry of the gulls outside the port-holes of the cabin.

Quite suddenly Lord Castleford was alerted to something which arrested his attention. He had no idea what it was; he only knew with some perception that he could not explain that his eyes were turned to the painted trunk on the other side of the cabin.

Jenkins had undone the two gold locks and pulled back the lid. From where he was sitting Lord Castleford could see a splash of crimson silk and what looked like the glitter of gems.

Then, as his eyes rested on it, incredibly and astonishingly the silk began to move!

At first it rushed through his mind that what he had been given was an animal or bird of some sort, but then the silk moved upwards and a moment later was pushed back to reveal a woman's face!

Lord Castleford could only stare, thinking that what he was seeing was a figment of his imagination. Then slowly, because she was cramped, Yamina rose to her feet.

She stood there in her rose-pink *entari*, the gauze chemise soft against the whiteness of her skin, and the precious stones of her girdle and stomacher-clasp flashing in the light coming through the port-holes.

Slowly she pushed back the veil from her head to reveal the diamonds glittering in her dark hair.

For a moment Lord Castleford found it impossible to move. Then he rose to his feet, exclaiming as he did so:

"What the devil do you think you are doing here?"

He spoke so violently that his voice seemed to echo round the cabin, and in his astonishment he spoke in English.

"I am sorry! It was the only way I could escape," Yamina said in the same language.

Lord Castleford walked towards her as she still stood in the trunk, the brilliant silks and satins with which Mihri had covered her encircling her legs with waves of colour.

"I know you! I have seen you before!" Lord Castleford said. "You are Yamina—the woman I rescued in the Bazaar!"

"I am flattered that Your Lordship should remember me!"

"But you have come from the Sultan's Palace!"

Then as if for the first time he realised how she was dressed, he looked her up and down, observing the veil which still covered her shoulders and the gauze chemise open to the waist.

"I had to . . . hide in the . . . Palace," Yamina said in a low voice.

She knew as she spoke that he was not only astonished at her appearance but also very angry.

There was a frown between his eyes and there was a note in his voice that she had not heard when they had met before.

"Then the sooner you return there, the better!" Lord Castleford said harshly. "You must be well aware that you cannot stay here on this ship with me."

"I realise it will be . . . difficult," Yamina replied, "but I really had no . . . alternative."

"What were you doing in the Palace," he enquired, "and dressed like that?"

"As I have already explained," Yamina replied, "I was hiding there."

"From what and from whom?" Lord Castleford enquired. "You did not appear to be hiding from anyone when I first met you."

There was a moment's silence. Then raising her chin a little, her eyes on his, Yamina said:

"I am a Russian!"

"Good God!"

The words seemed to be jerked from his lips. Lord Castleford turned to walk across the cabin and stand at the desk Jenkins had arranged for him in front of a port-hole, as if somehow it gave him support.

Yamina did not move. She just stood looking at him and after a moment he said:

"A Russian! And now you tell me you have escaped from the Sultan! What the hell am I expected to do about that?"

He paused, and as she did not speak he said:

"I imagine, if I ask the Captain to do so, he will stop the ship and we can set you down on Turkish soil."

"If you do," Yamina said, "doubtless the people will treat me in the same way as they treated the Russian we saw in the Bazaar."

After a short silence Lord Castleford turned round and said:

"What is the alternative? How can I possibly explain your presence here to anyone, especially when the ship is full of soldiers who have been wounded by your countrymen?"

Yamina did not reply, and after a moment he said more angrily:

"Can you imagine a worse situation for me than to find myself harbouring one of the enemy, and furthermore a member of the Sultan's Harem, whose escape might have far-reaching repercussions?"

"That is why it would be best," Yamina said quietly, "for no-one to learn I am here."

"How is that possible?" Lord Castleford snapped.

"I heard your Valet say that you were having your food in this cabin. Perhaps it would be wisest, if you can trust him, to take him into your confidence, but no-one else on board ship need know of my existence. When we reach Athens I can be set ashore with the rest of your luggage and disappear."

Lord Castleford did not reply and after a moment Yamina went on:

"I am afraid I shall have to ask you for a little ready money until I am able to sell some of my jewels, but I promise you will be reimbursed for anything you lend me."

There was a faint touch of irony in her voice, and now Lord Castleford said furiously:

"You have thought it all out, have you not? Well, I assure you, I will not be part of anything so underhand or ridiculous! Do you really imagine that I can arrive in Athens—the British Minister—bringing with me an exotic houri who is in fact one of England's enemies?"

"I admit it would be difficult to explain if anyone heard about it," Yamina answered, "but what I am suggesting is that no-one need know."

"You intend to stay here in my cabin?" Lord Castleford asked incredulously.

"Why not?" Yamina enquired. "If you are afraid, you can lock me in the trunk!"

There was something scathing in the way she spoke which made him look even more angry than he had before.

"The whole thing is preposterous, absurd, incredible!" he declared. "Who would believe I was completely innocent if there was even a whisper in diplomatic circles that I had travelled to Athens accompanied by a woman in a trunk?"

"That is why we must be very careful," Yamina agreed.

"We? We?" he said. "What have I done to be embroiled in this deplorable situation? And what is the Sultan going to say when he finds you have vanished?"

He paused to say almost apprehensively:

"Naturally you will be missed, and it will not be very difficult for anyone to guess how you escaped."

"Sahin, the White Eunuch who gave you the key of the trunk, and Mihri, who is the Sultan's favourite, are both Circassians, and were once in my father's service in our home at Balaclava. They helped me, knowing that had I been discovered in Constantinople I should have been torn to pieces by the mob!"

"There must have been other ways of protecting you!" Lord Castleford snapped.

"None that we could think of," Yamina said.

"You told me you were looking after your sick father," he said accusingly.

"I was," Yamina answered, "but my father died, and because a house-to-house search was taking place in the City, my Turkish servant who had been hiding us ever since we left Russia took me to Mihri."

"It all sounds very plausible," Lord Castleford sneered. "You expect me to believe that that was the only reason for your choosing to accompany me on this voyage?"

Yamina stepped from the trunk onto the floor of the cabin before she replied:

"Do you really think I had any other motive, My Lord? I assure you, until I heard you speak on the quayside before you stepped aboard the Caique, I had no idea that it was you who had an interview with the Sultan before joining this ship."

"A very strange coincidence!" Lord Castleford said, and once again he was sneering.

"If you really believe I could have any wish to accompany an enemy of my country aboard a British ship you must be half-witted!"

There was no doubt now that she was as angry as he was, and they faced each other defiantly, their eyes dark with rage. Lord Castleford's lips were set in a hard line and his chin was square.

"I should send you back!" he said at length.

"You are unable to do that because of the scandal it would cause," Yamina retorted. "Besides, if you do, I shall excuse my action by claiming that you begged me to run away with you!"

"That is just the sort of thing I would expect you to say!" Lord Castleford said. "Who can trust a woman, least of all a Russian?"

Yamina seated herself on one of the arm-chairs.

"That sort of remark will get you no-where," she said calmly.

"I am just wondering whether to go to the Captain and tell him the truth," Lord Castleford replied. "He can keep you prisoner. I am sure a cabin is available somewhere, and when we reach Athens he can put you on a steamer which will return you to Constantinople."

"Why not drop me overboard?" Yamina asked defiantly. "Or, better still, hand me over to the soldiers. Most of them will not have seen a woman for some months. I am certain I will be welcome!"

"It would serve you right if I did exactly that!" Lord Castleford retorted.

"I agree," Yamina said disarmingly. "I do understand how annoying and upsetting this must be for Your Lordship, and while I dislike you as much as you dislike me, I assure you that the alternative to playing this trick on you was so frightening that I was already prepared to die rather than accept it."

"And what was that?" he asked gruffly, curious despite himself.

"The Kizlar Aga, the Black Eunuch, intended that I should join his Harem."

Yamina saw the expression in Lord Castleford's eyes as she spoke and realised that the idea really shocked him.

"You can hardly expect me to believe that the Sultan would have agreed to that!"

"I was not one of the Sultan's women," Yamina explained. "Mihri, his favourite, who at the moment pleases him to the exclusion of all others, gave me refuge by pretending I was her sister. I have never seen the Sultan and he has never seen me; but because the Black Eunuch wants a hold over Mihri, the favourite *Ikbal,* he intended I should become one of his slaves."

Lord Castleford walked across the cabin.

"Those are your problems," he said. "You cannot expect me to involve myself in anything so controversial, or indeed so explosive from the point of view of my career."

"I can understand that," Yamina replied. "That is

why I am suggesting that no-one need ever know of my presence here."

Lord Castleford moved backwards and forwards without speaking. Then he said:

"What else can I do but agree?"

"Nothing else," Yamina answered calmly.

"If it was ever questioned," Lord Castleford said, almost as if he spoke to himself, "one can hardly contemplate the scandal, the gossip, the innuendos!"

"That is why no-one must know! It should not be difficult."

"Difficult? Of course it will be difficult!" Lord Castleford contradicted. "And apart from anything else, I have no wish to have a woman with me in my cabin. I had hoped for some privacy and a chance to work."

"I promise I will be very unobtrusive."

Yamina looked round and after a moment said:

"What I suggest is that we lower the mosquito-nets over the bed, which will provide me with an excellent hiding-place if anyone should come in to see you unexpectedly."

"That is unlikely!"

"Your servant," Yamina went on, "can make you up a comfortable bed on the floor."

"Thank you!" Lord Castleford said sarcastically. "You are obviously extremely solicitous for my comfort!"

Yamina smiled and it now was a smile of sheer amusement.

"I assure you that most Oriental beds, which are really no more than cushions on the floor, are far more comfortable than the mattresses which Europeans consider so essential. But, if you prefer, you can have the bed and I will have the cushions."

"You talk as if we were setting up house together," Lord Castleford said disagreeably.

"That is exactly what we have to do, for the short time we are at sea," Yamina answered. "When we arrive at Athens, I will be disembarked with your luggage, and once we reach the Residency in safety I will disappear!"

"The Residency!" Lord Castleford gave a groan. "Can you imagine what I as the incoming British Minister shall look like, arriving with a Russian in Turkish dress? Incidentally, I consider that costume extremely indecent!"

"There are some other garments in the trunk," Yamina replied, "but I doubt if they include a crinoline or a fashionable bodice buttoned tightly to the neck!"

She spoke in a manner which made Lord Castleford utter an inarticulate sound of fury, as he walked towards one of the port-holes to stand looking out at the sunshine glimmering on the sea.

"I am sorry . . . I really am! I did not mean to make . . . trouble for anyone."

Yamina's voice was almost pleading, and after a moment he said with some difficulty:

"I must also apologise for being rude, but you have completely disconcerted me."

"That is indeed understandable, considering, as I well know, that your career is at stake," Yamina said. "But I promise, if you will help me, no-one will ever know that I was here."

"I hope that will be possible," Lord Castleford said and turned from the port-hole to look at her.

Angry though he still was, he had to admit to himself that she was lovely. Her dark eyes were very large in her pale face, and her long hair glittering with diamonds fell over her shoulders and reached nearly to her waist.

Her lips were crimson and her eyes darkened with kohl in the manner of all the women in the Harem, but instead of making her look bold it seemed somehow at variance with the sensitiveness of her perfect features and the expression in her eyes which Lord Castleford could not help knowing was one of innocence.

"You are very young," he said unexpectedly.

"I shall be nineteen next month."

"You must have suffered some disagreeable experiences since you left Russia."

He paused, then asked:

"Why did you leave?"

"My father and I were at our country-house at Balaclava when the invading Armies closed in on us."

"So you escaped?"

"Our Turkish servant, whom you saw with me when we were in the Bazaar, managed to get us aboard a troop-ship carrying the wounded to Scutari."

"Then you hid somewhere near where I left you the other afternoon?"

"It is a poor part of the City with few houses, and we were safe there until the authorities decided on a house-to-house search."

"I understand your predicament," Lord Castleford said.

He walked across the cabin to sit down opposite her in another arm-chair.

His eyes were on her face as he said:

"I rode in that part of the town the afternoon after I left you. I had a feeling we might meet again."

"I saw you."

"From your house?"

"No, I was carried past you in a chair which was taking me to the Dolmabahce Palace."

He looked at her in surprise, and she knew he did not remember seeing the chair and the deaf mutes. Then he said:

"There was a house on fire. I was half-afraid that you might have been involved in it."

She knew he was thinking that the fire might have been caused by those seeking out spies and her eyes met his as she said:

"Did you suspect my nationality?"

"Not at the time," he answered, "but afterwards I wondered. The man being lynched by the mob disturbed you so obviously and I could not put a name either to your looks or to your accent."

He paused and there was a faint smile on his lips as he said:

"It is usually Russians who are so proficient in languages."

"I thought," Yamina said after a moment, "as I passed you on your horse I might call out to you and beg you to help me. If I had, what would you have done?"

"Quite frankly, I do not know!" Lord Castleford replied. "So I am glad you did not ask me then. Now I am obliged to help you. It is impossible for me to refuse."

"You are obviously not pleased to be in this awkward position."

"I am going to Athens in the position of British Minister," Lord Castleford said. "It is not a moment to be confronted with a human problem which unless very discreetly and carefully handled may wreck my career."

"I will not do that to you."

"Nothing you said or did would be any help, once you were discovered," Lord Castleford said.

Once again there was a heavy frown between his eyes as he went on:

"I am not so foolish as not to realise that a great number of men would envy me, and no-one would believe for one moment that I had not invited you to share my cabin."

"I am as aware of that as you are," Yamina said, "and that is why we must be exceedingly circumspect. Perhaps it would be best for you not even to tell your Valet. Every time he comes into your cabin you can lock me in the trunk."

"I would trust Jenkins with my life," Lord Castleford said. "In fact I have often done so. It is essential that he should know, not only because he will bring us food, but also of course because he must make up the bed on which you have decided I shall sleep."

Again he spoke scathingly and Yamina said a little hesitatingly:

"I am only trying to be . . . practical about all this. Perhaps it would have been . . . better if I had been . . . drowned in the Bosporus. Then there would have . . . been none of this trouble for . . . you or for me."

"Do not be so ridiculous!" Lord Castleford said sharply. "The War will not last forever; then I imagine you can return home."

"I will return to Russia," Yamina agreed, "and I suppose something may be left of our house in Balaclava, but I doubt it!"

She did not say how frightening the future felt for her, without her father and mother and with really no home left to go to.

She had never cared for her relations, and the necessity of living with her Uncle or cousins was something which she had considered and then set on one side until she was forced to make a choice in the matter.

Whatever happened now, the future was rather bleak, and she felt that she was, to all intents and purposes, alone in the world.

It could never be the same without her father, without the companionship which had meant so much to both of them these last few years.

Her face must have been very expressive; for after a moment Lord Castleford said:

"It is always worrying to make decisions before one has to. Let us concern ourselves for the moment with trying to get out of this mess. I cannot help feeling that we ought to be intelligent enough not to make any mistakes and above all not to be discovered!"

"My father used to say there was no problem the mind could not solve," Yamina said.

"I agree with him," Lord Castleford answered, "and that is why we must plan everything carefully. We must take no chances of any sort, and most of all we must never be taken by surprise."

As he spoke he walked across the cabin to shoot home the bolt on the inside of the door.

"The stewards have duplicate keys," he said as if in explanation. "It would be easy for them to enter at any time. It is essential that we always remember to bolt ourselves in."

"Yes, of course," Yamina agreed.

She too rose from the arm-chair and walked to the port-hole to look out, not to sea but upwards, as if she suspected that someone might lower himself from an upper deck and look in on them.

"I think we are safe from prying eyes," Lord Castleford said with a little smile.

"I hope so," Yamina replied. "But sailors climb about on ropes and there is always the chance that they might look in while doing so."

"I think it is unlikely," Lord Castleford said. "However, we must keep our voices low unless I wish to explain to anyone outside that I talk to myself!"

"Which is a sign of madness!"

"I admit to feeling that I was going a little mad when I first saw the silks moving in the trunk. I thought my present from the Sultan's favourite might be an animal or a bird of some sort."

"I am only hoping that those who saved me so cleverly will not get into trouble," Yamina said.

"You said your accomplice is the Sultan's favourite?"

"She is a Circassian and very beautiful," Yamina explained. "She was my maid in Balaclava and was kidnapped by the Sultan's Agents."

She saw that Lord Castleford was interested and went on:

"The White Eunuch who spoke to you and gave you the key of the trunk was also in my father's service. He also was abducted nine years ago. He has altered a great deal since."

"Eunuchs do," Lord Castleford said, "and the cruelty of it appals me!"

Yamina gave a little shiver.

"Even now I can hardly believe that I have escaped! Better, far better, to be a prisoner-of-war of the English than to have to stay in the Harem. Every moment I was there made me more and more frightened."

"I expect you will go down in history as one of the few women who ever escaped from a Sultan's Harem," Lord Castleford said.

"I was there in somewhat exceptional circumstances," Yamina replied. "An inmate, but not really one of the Sultan's women."

"Which means, I hope, that there will not be too fervent a search for you. Otherwise sooner or later someone will guess why I was given the painted trunk as a gift."

"I have thought of that," Yamina said, "and I cannot bear to contemplate Mihri or Sahin being punished on my behalf!"

There was such a note of horror in her voice that it made Lord Castleford say quickly:

"Forget about it! It will not do to torture yourself. What is done is done, and now if we are to survive we must concern ourselves with making sure no one has any suspicion that you are aboard the *Himalaya*."

"I am well aware of that."

"I still find it hard to believe that quite involuntarily I should find myself in such a predicament," Lord Castleford said. "I cannot help wondering what His Excellency, the Ambassador, would do in similar circumstances."

"I am sure he would think of something," Yamina said. "My father has often spoken of Lord Stratford and commended the reforms he has tried to make in the Ottoman Empire. It is a name that everyone respects in the East."

"He is a very wonderful man!" Lord Castleford agreed. "At the same time, he has never been involved in a scandal of any sort, despite the fact that he is so handsome."

"And you?" Yamina enquired. "Have you found yourself in awkward situations arising from your appearance?"

There was no doubt of the touch of sarcasm in her voice, and Lord Castleford replied bitterly:

"Never! I have thought far too much of my career to risk behaving in a manner which could bring any discredit to it or to my good name."

Yamina smiled.

"You sound very positive," she said. "Perhaps because you are so conscientious your life has been rather dull."

"I hardly think that is something they will say about me when they come to write my biography."

"I was not thinking about your biography; I was thinking about yourself. How many adventures, My Lord, have made your heart beat quicker and made you feel that the excitement and thrill counter-balanced the risk and even your fear of the consequences?"

"I have a feeling that you are talking not about exploits of bravery but of love," Lord Castleford said. "So let me tell you that love does not enter very greatly into my life. I am far too preoccupied with more important matters."

"More important?" Yamina queried.

"Much more important!" he replied. "It is hard for a woman to understand, I suppose, but for a man, if he has any intelligence, the most important objectives in his life are the achievements he attains mentally rather than physically."

"That is a very English point of view," Yamina said. "Most Russians are guided by their hearts and it is their hearts that point the way to the stars. For a man to be complete in himself he must be inspired."

"The achievements of the British, especially since the beginning of this century, speak eloquently for themselves," Lord Castleford replied, "and let me inform you that those achievements were accomplished by men who used their intellect, and were not swept off their feet by sheer emotion."

Yamina laughed.

"Such an argument is irrefutable, My Lord! At the same time, we were talking about you, not the British Empire, and I cannot help feeling that despite all you have achieved . . . and sometime I hope you will tell me about it . . . you still miss a great deal."

Lord Castleford remembered that the Ambassador had said very much the same thing, and because the idea irritated him he said crossly:

"I promise you I am entirely satisfied with my life as it is. I have no desire to be emotionally involved in dangerous or difficult situations, any more than I wish to be involved in the situation in which I now find myself."

"If I were a man it would be much easier, would it not?" Yamina asked.

"Much easier!" he agreed. "I could then hand you over to the Captain of this ship and wash my hands of you."

"He might be a little more human then you are," Yamina ventured provocatively.

"He would undoubtedly find you very alluring in that fancy-dress," Lord Castleford conceded. "And your appearance would doubtless please the men who, as you have already said, have not seen a woman for some months."

He meant to be scathing and succeeded; but when he saw the colour creep up her face he felt ashamed.

He pulled his watch from his waist-coat pocket.

"It is nearly four o'clock," he said. "My Valet will be bringing me tea. I think we had better be prepared with the story we intend to tell him!"

Yamina looked away, then said:

"You may perhaps think it cowardly of me, but I suggest you do not mention the fact that I am a Russian. Why not say that I was abducted unwillingly to the Sultan's Harem and that some friends inside the Palace contrived my escape?"

Lord Castleford did not speak and after a moment she said quickly:

"It is not that I am ashamed of my nationality . . . make no mistake about that! I am proud of being Russian . . . very proud! At the same time, it would be hard for anyone travelling together with a number of wounded men not to resent an enemy in their midst."

"I dare say you are right," Lord Castleford conceded. "I will tell Jenkins the story you have suggested, but while I tell him I think it best that you should not be present."

"I will go into the bath-room," Yamina said, "and I will not come out until you call for me."

She rose as she spoke and going to the trunk she pulled out one or two of the garments that Mihri had laid on top of her.

She found a caftan of *hembra,* which was velvet brocade woven with silver thread.

She took it with her into the bath-room and closed the door. As she did so Lord Castleford heard a key turn in the lock of the cabin-door and he pulled back the bolt.

Jenkins came in carrying a tray on which there was a pot of tea, a china cup, and a plate of sweet-biscuits which Lord Castleford recognised as having come from the Embassy.

The Valet set the tray down on a table, and when he had done so Lord Castleford said:

"Shut the door, Jenkins, I wish to speak to you."

He obeyed, then as he waited Lord Castleford said, choosing his words with difficulty:

"I have had a surprise, Jenkins."

"Indeed, M'Lord?"

"Yes! In the trunk which I brought from the Sultan's Palace there was not the present I had expected, but a young girl who had found it the only method of escape from the Harem!"

"A young girl, M'Lord?"

Even Jenkins, usually so phlegmatic, was astonished.

"She had been taken there against her will by the Sultan's Agents," Lord Castleford explained. "This was the only way she could escape and, as you can well understand, it is a considerable embarrassment to me!"

"Yes, indeed, M'Lord. What does Your Lordship intend to do about it?"

"There is nothing I can do, Jenkins, except take

this young woman to Athens and then somehow smuggle her out of the Residency."

Lord Castleford paused, then said slowly and impressively:

"You can understand better than anyone else, Jenkins, what trouble I should be in if this were discovered."

"You would indeed, M'Lord!"

"It would be impossible for me to protest that I was entirely innocent in the matter. No-one would believe that I had not been an accomplice in furthering the escape of one of the Sultan's women."

"I quite see that, M'Lord."

"And therefore, Jenkins, you will have to help me keep this secret until we are safe in the Residency in Athens."

"I understand, M'Lord."

"Fortunately I am having my meals here and you are waiting on me," Lord Castleford went on. "There should therefore be no reason for anyone else to enter the cabin."

"That's true, M'Lord."

"I feel I can trust your discretion and your cooperation," Lord Castleford said.

"You can trust me, M'Lord," Jenkins said stoutly.

"If anyone should insist for some reason upon coming into my cabin," Lord Castleford said, "Miss Yamina must go into the trunk. Otherwise she can hide, as she is now, in the bath-room."

Automatically Jenkins picked up a silk scarf which had fallen to the ground from the trunk when Yamina had left the cabin, folded it, and put it back inside.

"It'll not be difficult, M'Lord," he said after a moment.

"There will be the question of extra food."

Jenkins gave Lord Castleford an almost impish grin.

"They'll just think Your Lordship has a large appetite! As to additional cups and plates, leave them to me, M'Lord."

"I am sure I can do just that," Lord Castleford said.

Without being the least impertinent, Jenkins glanced towards the bed and Lord Castleford followed the direction of his eyes.

"You will let down the mosquito curtains," he said. "Miss Yamina will sleep there and you must somehow contrive to bring me some extra pillows. They can be placed on the floor for me to sleep on—Eastern-fashion."

As he spoke he thought it was annoying that Yamina had thought of the solution and he was obliged almost slavishly to follow it.

"I'll see to it, M'Lord," Jenkins said, "and if Your Lordship will excuse me, I'll go and fetch another cup."

"Will they not think that strange?" Lord Castleford asked hastily.

"Oh, no, M'Lord! Not if I tell them I dropped and broke this cup. And when no-one is looking I'll bring extra plates and cutlery in here so that there will be no questions asked when I am in the galley."

"Thank you, Jenkins. I knew I could leave everything with confidence in your hands."

"You can indeed, M'Lord."

He glanced towards the bath-room as if he was curious, then left the cabin.

Lord Castleford waited and after a few minutes Jenkins returned with another cup, which he set down on the tray.

"Is there anything else you require, M'Lord?"

"Nothing, thank you," Lord Castleford replied.

When his Valet had left the cabin he bolted the door behind him.

As if this was the signal she had been waiting for, Yamina came from the bath-room and Lord Castleford knew she had been listening.

She had changed from her elaborate and revealing Turkish dress and was now wearing the blue caftan in which she looked extremely beautiful. It was edged at the neck and sleeves with pearls and turquoises, and pearls were also embroidered in the silver on the velvet.

She had not taken the diamonds from her hair, which was still loose over her shoulders, and as she walked towards Lord Castleford he thought she might have stepped out of a Persian mosaic.

"I thought you managed that very skilfully," she said.

"I am of course gratified by your approval!" he replied sarcastically.

She gave him an amused smile and asked:

"Are you still very angry?"

"Naturally!" he replied. "At the same time, I find it exhausting to lose my temper, and a Diplomat should always be self-controlled."

"You were certainly not that when you first saw me in the trunk!"

"Can you be surprised?"

"Not really," she answered, "and I think perhaps I am delighted to have disturbed your British calm and broken through that pose of aloof indifference for which your countrymen are famed."

"Is that what you think about us in Russia?" he asked.

"But of course!" Yamina replied. "Nothing really provokes an Englishman into losing his temper—except, of course, a . . . woman!"

"You can congratulate yourself on being so successful!" Lord Castleford said. "Perhaps it would have been more effective if I had been icily calm."

"That actually was what I expected!" Yamina said. "I am quite relieved to find you are human after all!"

"Perhaps occasionally it is a good idea to see oneself through the eyes of the enemy," he said. "Although I must say the hospitality I received when I was last in Russia gave me a very different picture of myself from the one you are depicting."

"The Russians are a hospitable people and always

courteous," Yamina said. "Now we are at war, you can learn a few home truths."

"Would you really wish me to speak the truth?" Lord Castleford asked.

"Not if it means that you will be any more unpleasant than you have been already," Yamina said. "It will be hard to forget that you called me an 'exotic houri'!"

Lord Castleford smiled.

"Shall I tell you that at the moment you do not now look in the least like one?" he asked. "In which case I may be forgiven!"

"And I hope I do not look indecent.

"Shall I apologise?" he enquired.

"Do not trouble," she replied. "It is not what people say but what they do that matters, and therefore I am extremely grateful to you for not handing me over to the Captain."

"It would be a debatable point whether you should be a prisoner of the Navy or the Army."

"But instead, as your prisoner, I am safe from everything except your insults!"

Lord Castleford threw back his head and laughed.

"I see that, when it comes to repartee, you can hold your own," he said. "May I offer you, not a pipe of peace, but a cup of tea?"

"I accept, as long as it is without prejudice," Yamina said, "and I admit to feeling very much in need of something to eat and drink."

"You had no midday meal?"

"I am afraid I missed it, and a Turkish breakfast is not very sustaining."

"Let me order you something more substantial than these biscuits," Lord Castleford suggested.

Yamina shook her head.

"I shall look forward to dinner and I imagine that on board you will not dine late."

"I will order it early," Lord Castleford said, "and I promise you my Valet is a very good cook."

"I gathered that from the conversation you had with

him when we first came aboard," Yamina said. "You certainly travel in comfort, My Lord."

"I have never thought there is any particular merit in being uncomfortable when it is unnecessary," Lord Castleford replied.

"So you make yourself self-sufficient with your Valet, who can cook and look after you so efficiently that you do not need a wife?"

"That is what I have told myself," he said. "We have an adage in England which says: 'He travels fastest who travels alone.' "

"And you are very anxious to reach your goal. And what is it? . . . the Embassy in Paris?"

Lord Castleford looked surprised at her perception and Yamina smiled.

"My father knew a number of European Diplomats in St. Petersburg," she said, "and they always talked as if Paris was the El Dorado for which they all yearned."

"It is undoubtedly the most desirable and most important post to be bestowed by a benevolent Foreign Office," Lord Castleford said.

"So that will be your appointment after Athens?"

He hesitated for a moment as if he had no wish to confide in her. Then reluctantly he said:

"I am hoping so."

"That means you have a very good idea it will!" Yamina insisted. "Unless of course you blot your copybook in the meantime, which is what undoubtedly a houri in your luggage would do!"

"I have apologised for the description," Lord Castleford said.

"It still hurts a little."

"Words should never hurt us when they are untrue."

"But they do," Yamina said. "That is what is always so unfair in the world. It is the things which are not true, or rather half-true, which hurt so much more than downright lies."

She paused before she went on:

"For instance, however much you may know of the circumstances, however much I may explain them to you, you will always think of me as a woman from the Sultan's Harem—an odalisque—waiting to catch the eye of her Turkish Master."

Lord Castleford smiled.

"I thought when you walked across the room just now that you looked as if you had stepped straight from a Persian fifteenth-century mosaic, or perhaps from one of the Persian paintings on ivory which are so exquisite and so valuable that the Shah in Teheran has them specially guarded."

"I am flattered!"

"Looking as you do, how could you possibly have got yourself into such a situation that you are alone in the world without a family, parents, even a husband to take care of you?" Lord Castleford asked.

"It is just something that happened unavoidably," Yamina answered, "and that is why I am at this moment grateful that, whether you were willing to do so or not, you are taking care of me."

She gave a little shiver, half-real, half-pretence, before she added:

"I am on enemy soil, having tea with an enemy of my country; and yet it is not half so frightening as being in a Turkish Harem, looking over my shoulder for the approach of the Black Eunuch!"

Chapter 6

Yamina awoke with a sudden start, then remembered with a sense of relief that she was no longer in the Harem.

Instead she was now in the *Himalaya*, being carried away from all that was frightening in Turkey to an unknown and uncharted future which might be even more terrifying.

Nevertheless, she told herself in that strange state between waking and sleeping, for the moment she was safe.

Then she realised that she was not alone in the cabin and that Lord Castleford was lying on the floor on the pile of cushions with which Jenkins had made him up a bed.

It was, Yamina felt sure, quite comfortable, and while he looked at it somewhat disaparagingly she was certain it was more because he was determined to find fault than that he had any genuine grievance.

Now listening to the whirr of the engines and feeling the soft swell of the sea, she thought how strange it was that divided only by the mosquito-net which covered her bed she was in fact sleeping in the same room as a strange man who hated her as she hated him.

Then she asked herself if this was really true.

When Lord Castleford had come from the bathroom after changing for dinner she thought it would be hard to find a man who looked more elegant and more distinguished than he did in his evening-clothes.

Jenkins had laid the table and, the sea being calm, he had set a candelabra in the centre of it containing three candles.

At first they had no need for them, then as dinner was finished except for the coffee and they still sat talking, Jenkins had lit the candles and drawn the curtains over the port-holes to shut out the last glimmer of the sinking sun.

It was extraordinary, Yamina had thought, that she was conversing in a very civilised manner with the man who had raged at her earlier in the day and who was her enemy not only in view of his nationality but also because she had intruded upon his life.

And yet she realised that Lord Castleford was making a tremendous effort to ignore the awkward circumstances in which they found themselves.

Instead he talked to her of his travels, of his recent visit to Persia, which she had found absorbingly interesting, and of some of the dangerous situations he had encountered during his diplomatic life.

Her large dark eyes were fixed on his face as he talked and it would have been difficult for any man not to be flattered by her attention or to fail to appreciate how lovely she looked.

"I am afraid that tonight, at any rate," she had said when Lord Castleford joined her for dinner, "I cannot offer you a change of wardrobe."

"You look very attractive!" he said.

Then as if he felt he had been too complimentary he added:

"As I am quite certain you fully realise."

Yamina looked at him from under her long dark lashes and there had been a hint of amusement in her eyes.

"It is a pity to spoil such a pretty speech," she said, "and quite an eloquent one for an Englishman!"

Lord Castleford had laughed.

"You are quite determined to make me, and all my countrymen, obnoxious!" he said. "Perhaps one day we will surprise you when you least expect it."

"While you were dressing I was wondering what you are like when you are not on your guard," Yamina said. "You give me the impression that you are always afraid your words will be misconstrued or perhaps listened to by unauthorised persons. Therefore you choose them as carefully as another man chooses his wines."

"Perhaps that is a rather good description of what it means to be a Diplomat," Lord Castleford said.

"Surely you find it somewhat restricting?" Yamina suggested. "Do you never long to run wild, to say anything that comes into your head, to be completely natural and very, very undiplomatic?"

"I am trained to be self-controlled," Lord Castleford replied.

Then meeting Yamina's eyes he laughed again.

"I admit that when you first appeared out of that trunk you took me unawares. But I think, if you are honest, you prefer me when I discipline both my tongue and my anger."

"I will tell you the answer to that assumption," Yamina replied, "when we have grown to know each other a little better."

It was something which had already begun to happen, she thought, by the end of dinner.

She had never before dined alone with a man other than her father, and she found it an experience that was definitely intriguing.

It seemed to her that as she and Lord Castleford sat at the table in the centre of the cabin they were, as it were, on an island by themselves.

Outside, there was, to all intents and purposes, an angry and dangerous sea.

For the moment they were isolated, two people who had been brought together by fate and who in consequence could not help exploring each other as if they were each of them a piece of unknown land.

"We are without maps, without compasses, without anything but our own instincts to tell us what is true or false," Yamina told herself.

She smiled without realising it, so that Lord Castlefore said:

"Tell me what is amusing you?"

"Us!" Yamina answered truthfully. "The fact that we are here together knowing nothing of each other personally, and yet undoubtedly prejudiced because we are on opposite sides of a war!"

"I see what you are trying to say," he replied, "and that is why war is wrong, unnecessary, and completely primitive!"

He looked across the table at Yamina and said:

"When I was in St. Petersburg four years ago I was entertained royally by the Tsar and many distinguished Russians. I liked to think I had made many real friends amongst them. Yet because a Russian Ambassador chose to be deliberately aggressive and needled the Turks into defiance, I have lost friendships I should have valued all my life."

"The situation is absurd if one thinks about it like that," Yamina agreed, "but I am sure when the War is over you will be able to go back to Russia and pick up the threads where you left off."

"I wonder if that will be possible?" Lord Castleford said reflectively.

"I am sure it will be," Yamina replied. "It may take a little time, but that is what happens when one becomes involved in international events."

"No, that is what happens when Governments use force instead of diplomacy!"

"So you look upon yourself as a man of peace?"

"I do indeed!" he answered.

Yamina raised her glass.

"Then I drink to your future!" she said. "For all women seek peace and hate war!"

They talked at the table until Jenkins came to take away the coffee-cups and leave a decanter of port and a glass beside one of the arm-chairs for Lord Castleford.

They sat on talking and duelling with each other verbally, until, without meaning to, Yamina's eye-lids drooped a little and she stifled a yawn.

"You are tired," Lord Castleford said. "It has been an exhausting day for you, and one which involved you in many conflicting emotions—the worst, I imagine, being fear!"

Yamina thought of how fearful she had been while being carried from the Harem; of the fear she had experienced thinking she might be discovered before the Caique left the steps of the Palace; and again of the fear that Lord Castleford might forget his present and she would not be taken aboard the *Himalaya*.

Now the fears had gone but she was still suffering from reaction.

"Go to bed," Lord Castleford said.

She thought his voice was kind and he added:

"I am going on deck and I shall be away for at least an hour."

Yamina rose to her feet and he rose too.

They stood for a moment looking at each other and it seemed to her that although they were not speaking they still were communicating. Something indeed was still being said, and yet she was not certain what it was.

"Good-night, Yamina!"

Lord Castleford turned and went from the cabin, shutting the door carefully behind him.

Yamina undressed and got into bed.

She expected she would find it difficult to go to sleep before Lord Castleford came back, but actually she was only vaguely conscious of his return, when he was somehow part of her dreams.

But now she was abruptly aroused from her sleep by hearing the engines stop and the anchor being lowered.

For a moment she was afraid. What could have occurred? Could anything have happened to make them turn back and not proceed on the journey as planned?

Thoughts rushed through her mind and without meaning to she sat up in bed.

Lord Castleford must have been aware of her movement because he too roused himself and said:

"Do not be alarmed, Yamina. I learnt from the Captain that we were to stop at Monte Santo. One of the Russian monks from a famous Monastery on Mount Athos was wounded while ministering to the soldiers in the Crimea. They intend to land him here."

"Monte Santo!" Yamina exclaimed. "How I wish it was daylight and I could see it! They say that the Virgin Mary stayed here for some time and for centuries no woman has been allowed to contaminate the Holy Mountain."

"It may be a legend in which the Monks believe," Lord Castleford said, "but actually five years ago Lord Stratford and his wife visited Monte Santo and Lady Stratford was entertained in one of the Monasteries."

"Once again, the intrusive female influence where it was least expected," Yamina said with laughter in her voice.

Lord Castleford had risen as he was speaking, and having put on a long robe which Jenkins had left for him over a chair he walked to the nearest port-hole and drew back the curtains.

Instantly moonlight, silver and brilliant, flooded in and Yamina could see him silhouetted against it.

"Come and look," he suggested, "then you will have no regrets at not seeing Monte Santo in the day-time."

"I would like to do that!" Yamina exclaimed.

He heard her moving about behind the mosquito-netting before she asked:

"Will you shut your eyes?"

"Why?" Lord Castleford enquired.

"Because," she replied, "it is very difficult to put on a caftan sitting on a bed. It would be far easier for me if I stood up."

There was a pause, then he asked:

"Are you telling me that you are sleeping naked?"

"Does that shock you?" Yamina enquired. "As a matter of fact, it was unavoidable simply because my friend, Mihri, has sent me with nothing but expensive and elaborate garments all embroidered with pearls and precious stones."

She gave a little laugh.

"I tried, when I first got into bed, sleeping in the thinnest and lightest of them, but I felt exactly like the Princess in the fairy-tale who could feel a pea under twelve mattresses! Only in my case it was not a pea but a large number of pearls which were extremely painful!"

"I am not complaining," Lord Castleford said. "I was only interested!"

"Your eyes are shut?"

"I can see nothing!" he replied.

He heard a rustle as Yamina stepped out of bed. Then involuntarily, without thought, he opened his eyes.

In the moonlight he saw something so exquisite, so perfect, so unbelievably lovely, that he felt he was looking at one of the Greek goddesses come to earth to bemuse a mortal man.

Then as Yamina slipped her arms into the caftan which she held high above her head it slithered down over her body.

Throwing back her long hair, she walked across the cabin towards him.

As she did so Lord Castleford realised she was wearing a garment of gauze embroidered with pearls and tiny diamonds so that she seemed, as it caught the moonlight, to be arrayed in stars.

She came to his side, looked out through the port-hole, and gave an exclamation of delight.

The cone-shaped mountain rose high in front of them, the lower slopes of it covered with groves of Spanish chestnut trees and forests of oaks and pines.

There were glimpses too of the white buildings of the mediaeval Monasteries of the Orthodox Church. Everything was bathed in a silver light that gave the scene a mystery and a beauty that was indescribable.

"It is lovely! More lovely than I believed anything could be!" Yamina exclaimed.

She stood looking and it was difficult to speak.

In front of them, the sea glimmered against the rocky slopes and the grey precipices, while the top of Monte Santo seemed to be haloed with the light of the gods.

"I shall always remember this!" she said.

As she spoke she realised that Lord Castleford was not looking at the mountain but at her.

She raised her eyes enquiringly, then was held spell-bound by the expression in his.

For a moment they stood staring at each other, while his eyes took in the purple darkness of her hair falling over her shoulders and the shimmer of the garment she wore, which did not conceal the soft curves of her breasts or her neck rising like a white column to hold the grace of her head.

Then, as they still stood immobile like statues, Yamina's lips parted a little and it was difficult for her to breathe.

Suddenly, violently, so that his voice seemed to split the silence between them as if he had cracked a whip, Lord Castleford ejaculated:

"For God's sake, do not look at me like that!"

Even as he spoke he put out his arms and drew Yamina roughly, crushingly, against him so that she felt the impact jar her.

Then his lips were on hers, hard, cruel, almost brutal in their insistence.

For a moment she could feel nothing except the pain of them! Vaguely, far away at the back of her mind, she felt she must struggle, and yet she was unable to move.

Then a strange feeling rose within her that she had never known before.

It was a sensation which sprang from her lips and yet pervaded her whole body, and she knew as she felt it that Lord Castleford's possession of her mouth was not so cruel nor so hard, but still demanding, so that he held her captive.

She felt completely subservient to his will; something without the instruction of her brain made her surrender herself and become a part of him.

He held her still tighter, and yet his lips became tender, even gentle, but still masterful and completely and utterly possessive.

Yamina had thought during dinner that they were like two people alone on an island, but now they had become one in a world where nothing else existed except themselves. She thought that this must be how the gods would feel on Olympus and that here was the real meaning of ecstasy.

She could not move, she could hardly breathe, and yet her whole body responded to the wonder of his kiss and the demand of his lips.

She was conscious of his heart beating against her breast, and their bodies were so close to each other that it was hard to realise that they were two and not one.

Then with a sound that was half an exclamation, half a groan, as violently as he had taken her into his arms, Lord Castleford pushed her from him.

"Go back to bed while I can still let you!" he commanded harshly.

As Yamina with difficulty prevented herself from falling to the floor, he walked towards the door, opened it, and, leaving the cabin, slammed it behind him.

Yamina stood alone in the moonlight, feeling as if a bomb had fallen through the ceiling and everything had been turned upside-down.

For a moment it was impossible to think; she could only feel the inexpressible rapture which had swept through her body when he held her captive.

She could not translate its meaning even to herself; she only knew there was a throbbing within her breasts, her lips hurt from the violence with which he had kissed her, while at the same time they trembled with the wonder of it.

She turned to the port-hole and laid her cheek against the coolness of the glass, looking out onto the enchanted silver beauty of Monte Santo.

There was a sense of calm serenity in the landscape, but it did nothing to calm the tumult within Yamina.

Lord Castleford had awakened a rapture within her and now her body burned with a strange fire.

It was a fire that was part of the moonlight because it was the intensification of all beauty, and yet it was far more vulnerable and infinitely more human.

Because she felt he might return and would be angry to see that she had not obeyed him, she pulled the curtain over the port-hole and shut out the blinding beauty of the moon. Then moving across the cabin she crept beneath the mosquito-netting.

She slipped off the embroidered caftan, covered herself with the sheet, and shut her eyes.

She knew it was impossible to sleep. She could feel herself thrilling from the top of her head to the soles of her feet with the fire Lord Castleford had awakened.

She could not think of him coherently. He was no longer the man with whom she had talked at dinner or the man who had raged at her for involving him in her escape.

He was a god-like figure who had stepped into her life and made her a part of him.

This was what she had dreamt of, what she had

longed for without realising it, what she had known was waiting somewhere for her in the world, if only she could find it.

It was what she had never understood but which was written now in words of fire on her heart.

It was love!

* * *

It was dawn when Lord Castleford finally returned to the cabin.

He moved very softly and Yamina knew he thought she would be asleep.

He threw himself down just as he was on his cushioned couch and after a long while she thought he slept, but she was not sure.

Thinking of him, still overwhelmed with the new emotions he had evoked, she fell asleep and when she awoke it was to hear him in the bath-room.

He was taking a bath and she realised it was early in the morning and the ship was moving again.

He dressed himself without the help of his Valet, and a little later came from the bath-room, moving softly across the still-darkened cabin to leave through the outer door. Once again Yamina was alone.

She lay for a long time thinking about what had happened, then rising went to the bath-room to bathe and dress.

She had nothing to wear except the *entari* in which she had come aboard and which Lord Castleford had told her was indecent.

The only alternatives were the turquoise velvet caftan, which was far too warm, the one lined with sable, on which she had rested in the trunk, and several gossamer garments like the one she had worn last night, embroidered with diamonds and pearls.

With nothing beneath them Yamina thought they would be even more indecent in the day-time than the *entari*. So she put the *entari* on and searched in the trunk for something with which to fasten the gauze chemise at the neck.

It was that which had shocked Lord Castleford because it was open to the waist.

Fortunately she found that decorating the little round *talpock* she had worn on her head was a pearl-and-topaz brooch which matched her girdle and stomacher-clasp.

She took the brooch from the hat and pinned it to her chemise high at the neck. And in a further effort to appear more respectable she arranged her hair at the back of her head in a large chignon.

It was very difficult to do as she had no pins, but she managed with ribbons and the effect was, she hoped, more demure and lady-like than when her hair was falling over her shoulders.

She was dressed when Jenkins came into the cabin, bringing her breakfast.

"His Lordship's compliments, Miss," he said, "and he asked me to tell you that he has been invited to breakfast with the Captain."

As he spoke, Jenkins laid a clean cloth on the table and set down a tray on which there was coffee and a covered dish.

Yamina felt it would be impossible to eat, for she still had a strange constriction in her throat when she thought of Lord Castleford and what had happened last night.

But because Jenkins was present and she felt it might seem ungracious not to eat anything after he had taken so much trouble she played with the toast and honey which he had also brought on the tray.

"Will it disturb you, Miss, if I tidy the cabin?" the Valet enquired.

"No, of course not," Yamina replied.

Jenkins lifted up the cushions on which Lord Castleford had lain last night and Yamina saw there was also a mattress which he had procured in some magic manner of his own.

Having made her bed, he laid the mattress underneath it, while the extra cushions which went on top were concealed by the mosquito-net.

"It's just in case anyone pays His Lordship a visit, Miss," Jenkins explained. "It never pays to be 'caught napping'!"

"No, indeed!" Yamina agreed.

"Anything else I can get you, Miss?" Jenkins asked a little later when he had tidied the bath-room.

"No, thank you," Yamina replied.

She knew that she was waiting for Lord Castleford's return. She was not quite certain whether she was apprehensive, frightened, or eager.

It was difficult to sort out her feelings concerning him, and yet when several hours later he did come she knew exactly what would happen.

She was standing at the port-hole, looking out into the sunlight, hoping to catch a glimpse of the many islands they must pass as they moved through the Aegean Sea, when she heard the door open.

For a moment she did not move.

She knew who it was and heard him shut the door and bolt it. Then very slowly she turned round.

The sun was on his face and the expression in his eyes as he looked at her made her heart turn over in her breast.

Slowly he walked across the room and she waited for him as she felt she must have waited through all eternity.

He reached her. Then after a long moment he said:

"It is true! I thought I must have been dreaming!"

"What is . . . true?" she asked, her eyes on his.

"That you are more beautiful than I believed possible for any woman to be."

There was silence, before he said in a low voice:

"Last night I thought you must have been a goddess, but today I know you are human."

He drew in his breath, then he said:

"Yamina, what has happened? How could it be possible I should feel like this?"

"Like . . . what?" Yamina asked, and it was difficult to speak.

He did not touch her, and yet as his eyes lingered on her lips she felt as if he kissed her.

After a moment he answered:

"When I was in India I heard a man singing one night as I stood on the verandah of a bungalow up in the Hills."

Yamina's eyes were on Lord Castleford's face as he went on:

"I asked one of my friends to translate the words of the song and they were:

'To love or not, we are no more free
Than a ripple to rise and leave the sea.'"

There was silence, then Yamina asked:

"Is what you . . . feel . . . love?"

"I do not know," Lord Castleford replied. "If it is, I have never been in love before. The next lines of the song were:

'I am always the slave of this—
The burning fire of your lips' sweet kiss.'"

As he spoke he put out his arm slowly and drew Yamina towards him.

It was a movement so different in every way from the violence with which he had taken her last night. Now it was as if he calculated and savoured every moment.

Then as her head fell back against his shoulder his lips sought hers.

Again it was different from the night before, because his mouth was gentle and tender, almost as if he was wooing her.

Only as he felt the sudden fire in Yamina flicker into being did his lips become possessive, and once again demanding.

He kissed her until the world whirled round them and she was conscious of nothing but him. When at length he released her he said a little unsteadily:

"How can this be possible? How can it have happened to me of all people? I do not know. I never saw you until a few days ago, and yet now there is nothing in my life but you!"

"That is what I . . . feel too!" Yamina whispered. "But you are . . . right . . . it is . . . impossible! We can mean . . . nothing to each other!"

"What do you mean—nothing?" Lord Castleford demanded harshly.

Then he was kissing her again, half-angrily, roughly, demandingly, as he had done the night before.

Everything that was primitive in Yamina leapt to meet what was primitive in him.

They clung together, one person, until as if the wonder of it was too intense to be bearable. Yamina put up her hand and laid it against his lips.

"Please . . ." she begged, "please . . . do not . . . make me feel . . . like this."

"Like what?" he enquired.

Reluctantly, but knowing that she wanted it, he set her free.

She turned to hold on to the side of the port-hole, finding it hard to get her breath, feeling as if she were not only blinded but permeated with the glory of the sun outside.

"It is impossible to believe this has . . . happened . . . . but it has!" she said. "And yet we must . . . try to be . . . sensible."

"Sensible?" Lord Castleford questioned. "What do you suggest we do?"

"There is . . . nothing we can do," Yamina answered. "We arrive in Athens tomorrow and . . . after that we shall never . . . see each other again."

"Do you really believe that is possible?" Lord Castleford asked.

"It is not only possible," Yamina said, "it is what has to happen . . . but we must not make it worse. It will be difficult enough to say . . . good-bye to you."

"Difficult?" he repeated, with a sound that seemed to come from the very depths of his being.

When he would have put his arms round her again she resisted him, and moving across the cabin stood at the far end of it, her eyes very dark.

"Do I frighten you?" Lord Castleford asked.

"I am not frightened of you," Yamina said, "but no . . . that is not quite true . . . I am frightened of you and of myself . . . of both of us . . . together! It is as if we have . . . suddenly been plunged into a . . . whirlpool and now we do not know how to get out of it."

Lord Castleford put his hand up to his forehead.

"Yesterday I thought I hated you!" he said. "But I think now that it was fear, not anger, that I was experiencing."

Yamina did not speak and after a moment he went on:

"Your face had haunted me ever since we met in the Bazaar. I kept thinking about you, remembering the fragrance of the scent you use. It seemed to linger on my coat and I wanted to see you again."

"So you came to look for me," Yamina said softly.

"I told myself that I was behaving courteously to a lady in distress," Lord Castleford admitted, "but I know now it was a yearning need to look at you, to be certain you were as beautiful as I remembered."

He drew a deep breath before he said:

"I could still feel the softness of your body in my arms, although last night it was even softer and closer!"

Yamina made a little helpless gesture with her hand.

"How can this have . . . happened?" she asked. "How can we . . . feel like this? We are . . . enemies."

"Do you really believe that?" Lord Castleford asked.

For the first time there was a faint smile on his lips and a note of amusement in his voice as he went on:

"If enemies behaved like us, my lovely one, no war would last very long."

"It was just an explosion between us," Yamina said hastily. "We were both tense . . . both perhaps on edge. We must try to . . . forget what has happened, but you must not . . . touch me again."

"Do you really think I could ever forget?" Lord Castleford asked.

As he spoke he walked across the cabin towards her.

He came near to her as she watched him, her eyes on his. Then when he was about a foot away from her he said very softly:

"And do you really think it possible for us to stay here together and for me not to touch you?"

She did not answer, she only looked at him, but he knew she trembled.

"My darling!" he said very, very softly. "I am in love! I had no idea love was like this, but now I can think of nothing but you and how much I need you!"

He opened his arms as he spoke and for a moment Yamina strove to refuse him, until as if her need was irresistible she moved towards him and hid her face against his shoulder.

His arms went round her, he kissed her hair, then one hand went to the ribbons with which she had so painstakingly arranged her chignon.

He pulled her hair loose and it fell in luxuriant waves over her shoulders as if glad to be free of confinement.

Lord Castleford touched it and felt the silkiness of it with his fingers. Then he turned Yamina's face up to his and looked down into her eyes.

"I love you!" he said. "Those are words which have never come to my lips before, and now I want to keep on saying them. I love you! But you have not yet told me what you feel for me."

"I love you too!" Yamina whispered. "But it is hopeless . . . crazy . . . impossible! As far as you are concerned, something that is totally and completely . . . forbidden."

"That is for me to decide."

"You must be sensible."

"Is this sensible?" he asked almost savagely.

He kissed her forehead, her eyes, her cheeks, and then as she wanted him to kiss her lips more than she had ever wanted anything before in her life, his mouth was on hers!

He kissed her slowly, deliberately, and she felt as if he was more masterful and more possessive than he had been before.

It was as if he demanded from her not only her heart but also her soul; as if he wanted her to surrender her very thoughts so that she no longer had any identity of her own.

This was love . . . this was life . . . and an ecstasy like a brilliant light.

* * *

It was a long time later before they drew apart and Yamina, feeling curiously weak about the knees, sat down in one of the arm-chairs.

Her eyes were shining, her face was radiant, and Lord Castleford knew he had never seen a woman look so ecstatically happy.

Then as if she deliberately dragged herself back from the heights of bliss she said:

"You would be the first to say that we must not be . . . slaves to our . . . emotions . . . that we have to . . . consider what we are . . . doing."

She drew in her breath as she said:

"Tomorrow we shall arrive in Athens. I have to . . . leave you, and to be more . . . in love than I am at the moment will make it an . . . agony I cannot . . . contemplate."

"Then why think about it?" Lord Castleford asked.

"Because it is something we have to face."

"Let tomorrow take care of itself," he said. "We have today and tonight and somehow, when tomorrow comes, I will find a solution to our problems."

"Can you?" Yamina asked.

"I have no idea until I think about it," he answered. "At the moment I only want to think about you."

He gave her a smile as he said:

"I thought I was immune to love. I told Lord Stratford only two days ago that I would never be in the maudlin state where a man can no longer think clearly, when he believes the world is well lost for the sensations evoked in him which could not be anything but transient."

"Is that what you feel about us?" Yamina enquired.

"You know as well as I do that this is nothing that could be described as either maudlin or transient. It is something that has been there waiting for us since the beginning of time."

"Do you really . . . believe that?"

"I have lived too long in the East not to believe in Kismet, or fate," Lord Castleford replied, "and you, my precious, are my fate!"

There was a little twist to his lips as he said:

"Lord Stratford and a great number of other people would be amused to learn that it has caught up with me at last!"

"You were so sure of yourself . . . so confident . . . that you could remain . . . aloof and indifferent?" Yamina said.

"I did not know that you were waiting for me," Lord Castleford replied.

He looked at her as she sat opposite him and added:

"If I could have looked into a crystal ball and seen us at this moment, I suppose every instinct nurtured by my education and upbringing would have made me run away as hard as I could in the opposite direction."

He saw the sudden pain in her eyes and added quickly:

"You know that is not true! Do you think for one moment that I would willingly have missed what I am feeling now, or what I felt last night?"

"What did you do after you left me?" Yamina enquired.

"I walked round the deck," Lord Castleford said, "telling myself that what I felt for you was just passion, a physical desire because you were so beautiful."

"And . . . then?" Yamina prompted as he stopped speaking.

"Then I knew it was something very different," Lord Castleford said. "I knew you were mine, completely and absolutely mine, that no words or arguments can alter the fact that we belong to each other, and there is not only a physical bond between us but also a spiritual one."

"Do you really . . . mean that?" Yamina asked.

"I mean it!" Lord Castleford said. "And that is why, my darling, I know now that I cannot live without you."

Yamina rose from the chair to look once again out through the port-hole.

"It is no use talking like that," she said. "What do we know about each other? As you say, this may be just something physical, something, I understand, which happens between a man and a woman like a fire that is suddenly ignited but which can die down just as quickly."

"Is that what you feel about me?"

He had not moved, and yet she felt he was standing very close to her.

"Women are . . . perhaps . . . different," she said hesitatingly.

"I am not asking you about women," he said. "I am asking about you! Do you feel this is something that has burst into life and which once we separate will no longer trouble either of us?"

Yamina did not answer and after a moment he went on:

"That is what I have felt where other women were concerned. I wanted them, desired them; but once I had made them mine they were no longer of any particular importance. Sometimes our liaison, if that is the right word for it, continued; sometimes it died away the moment we were both satisfied."

There was something scathing in his voice and as Yamina still did not speak he said:

"Are you telling me that that is what you are feeling now?"

"N-no!" Yamina answered after a moment. "It

would be . . . sacrilege to decry anything so beautiful . . . so wonderful! I felt as if you carried me to the very top of Olympus. We were not human beings . . . but gods! It was a . . . rapture that was . . . divine!"

Lord Castleford rose from his chair to stand beside her.

"My beloved darling!" he said softly. "That is what I felt too. It was love as it is meant to be. Not a quiet, sentimental, sloppy emotion, but something great, stupendous—as mighty as the sea, as magnificent as a tempest, as invincible as the burning heart of the sun! That, Yamina, is what I feel for you!"

She turned towards him and as he put his arms round her he knew that she was trembling at the sudden ecstasy his words had evoked.

He looked down into her eyes.

"I love you!" he said very gently. "And that is why, my precious, I know that I cannot live without you, and for either of us to be complete we must be together!"

"It is . . . impossible!" Yamina said. "You must know that it is . . . impossible!"

He did not answer, he merely bent his head and found her lips and now they clung together like two children who had been frightened and could find security only by the touch and feel of the other.

Yamina's arms went round his neck and he held her closer and still closer, as if he was making her a part of himself and it was impossible for them to be divided.

Then there was a sound outside the door and they knew that Jenkins was bringing in their luncheon.

Slowly they moved apart.

For Yamina it was almost as if a sword separated them and the hurt of it was agony.

"How can I . . . leave him?" she asked herself. "Oh, God . . . how can I . . . leave him and face the future . . . alone?"

Chapter 7

Jenkins had excelled himself in his efforts to provide them with a delicious meal, and Lord Castleford had brought aboard with him a golden wine which tasted like liquid sunshine.

It was, however, difficult for Yamina to think of anything but the man sitting opposite her, knowing that when their eyes met it seemed as if the world stood still.

She wondered how she had ever thought him aloof and indifferent.

Now he seemed to her to vibrate with feeling and his voice had a new depth and warmth that had not been there before.

She had never imagined that it was possible to feel as she did and to know a new awareness which seemed to seep through her body and make her feel as if she had never been alive before.

She had dreamt of being in love: in Russia love was

a part of living; the music, the literature, the thought, the people themselves were all activated by love in one way or another.

Because Yamina had never been emotionally awakened, it had been for her like looking at a picture which, however beautiful, left one outside the subject it depicted.

Now she was inside, now she was completely involved in love, and it was different from anything she had expected or imagined.

She knew quite literally that she would be prepared to die for Lord Castleford if it was asked of her. But the problem was not to die, but to live without him.

At last luncheon was finished and Jenkins cleared the table, removed the coffee-cups, and left them alone.

Yamina rose from the table to go to the open porthole.

The sea was so smooth that there was no reason to have it closed, and the warm sun flooded into the cabin with a golden light.

There was the fragrance of flowers on the air and the sea was emerald green shading to an azure blue at the base of the distant islands.

It was all so exquisitely lovely and there was, Yamina thought, a difference in the quality of light from anywhere else she had ever been.

She was sure that it was the pure light of the gods which made the distant hills have a fragility about them, and the very air seemed full of the vibrations of light coming from another world.

She thought that if they came near enough to the islands that were so much a part of Greek mythology she would see one of the goddesses playing on a lyre, another on a flute, and a third on a shepherd's pipe.

She could almost hear the music coming to her across the water, and yet she knew that the melody was within herself because of her love and because Lord Castleford was near her.

He sat for a few minutes watching her, the sunshine

haloing her head, the perfection of her profile silhouetted against the sky. Then at last he said quietly:

"Come here, Yamina—I wish to talk to you."

"It is safer when I am not too near to you," she answered.

He smiled very tenderly as he replied:

"If by saying that you think you can escape me, you are wrong!"

"I am trying to think," Yamina said, "and it is impossible to think when I am close to you."

"There is no need for you to think," Lord Castleford said. "I have already decided everything! So come here, as I have asked you to do!"

She turned round slowly and saw that he was standing holding out his hand to her, and as if she could not help herself she ran towards him.

He gave a laugh of sheer happiness as he pulled her against him, then as he felt a quiver go through her he said:

"So sweet, so irresistible, so utterly and completely adorable!"

Her eyes dropped at the passion in his voice and her eye-lashes were dark against her white skin.

He did not kiss her, he only looked down at her face, holding her closely against his breast.

"Are you ready to hear my plans, my precious?" he asked.

"You know I will listen to everything you have to tell me," Yamina answered. "At the same time, I do not promise to agree to them if they should harm you in any way."

"It depends what you mean by harm!" Lord Castleford said. "The only thing that could really harm me is if I should lose you!"

She did not answer, but he knew she was tense until he said very quietly:

"That is why, my darling, we will be married as soon as I have sent in my resignation."

Yamina looked up at him, her eyes very wide and dark.

"No!" she said sharply. "No!"

She pulled herself from his arms and walking away from him stood holding on to the back of a chair, as if she needed support.

"Do you think I would really let you resign?" she asked. "Give up your career for me?"

"It is what I intend to do," Lord Castleford replied with a note of authority in his voice. "And I do not need your permission on that question, only as to whether you will honour me by becoming my wife!"

"Listen . . . please listen to me," Yamina pleaded frantically. "How can you even consider a step that would destroy everything you have worked for, everything for which you have been trained these past years?"

"I used to think my career was the most important thing in the world," Lord Castleford said, "but you have shown me that I was mistaken. I have never known happiness until this moment, Yamina. Do you imagine that I would throw it away wantonly and destructively?"

"Life is not like that," Yamina said. "To me, love is everything; you are my whole world! But for a man it is different."

"Most men think that happiness lies in their work," Lord Castleford answered. "That is what I believed myself until I met you. Now I know that work and success, the crowns of glory one achieves, are only a pale imitation of the happiness that comes from love."

"But supposing you did give up everything for me?" Yamina said. "And then if you found it was not enough, what would there be left? Misery, frustration, and an unavoidable bitterness."

"That might be true where most people are concerned," Lord Castleford replied, "but you and I are different, Yamina. This is not, as we both know, a transitory affection which, as you said yourself, is like a fire that bursts into flame, then dies away as quickly, leaving nothing but ashes. This is real, my darling."

"How can you be sure of that?"

"Are you not sure?"

"You know I am! But I have nothing to give up. There are no long years of hard work behind me, nor the spur of ambition which you have and which you cannot deny."

"I admit that in the past, ambition drove me hard," Lord Castleford agreed. "I was glad when I received Lord Palmerston's letter sending me to Greece simply because it was another step up the ladder. But now I am not interested in Greece or Paris or the Court of St. James. I only want you!"

"Do you think that I would be enough? How could one woman fill your mind to the exclusion of all else, even if she could satisfy your body?"

Lord Castleford smiled.

"You are very eloquent, my darling, but I assure you I am not a love-sick boy acting on the impulse of the moment. I have calculated exactly what this will mean. I have weighed up the consequences of my action, and I know irrefutably that I shall be doing the right thing, the only thing that matters to me, when I become your husband."

Yamina did not reply but her eyes were on his face and he saw them suddenly fill with tears.

"My sweet!" he said, and stepping across the space that divided them he took her into his arms.

She hid her face against his shoulder and he felt her tremble.

After a moment she said in a broken voice:

"I did not . . . know that any man could be so . . . wonderful! So utterly and . . . completely . . . magnificent!"

"You have never known a man who has loved you like I do," Lord Castleford said, "and you will never know another!"

His arms tightened.

"I shall be a very jealous husband!"

"I have not yet said that I will marry you," Yamina said. "After all, we know so little about each other. You may be disappointed when you know me better!"

"I know everything that matters," Lord Castleford said. "Perhaps anyone listening to us would think it strange that I do not know your name. It is of little consequence, but perhaps it is something of which I should have made a note."

He was smiling as he spoke, but Yamina was still and did not move her face from against his shoulder.

"One Russian name is very like another," she said. "What really matters is the fact that I am Russian, and to marry me, an enemy of your country, would be to throw away your diplomatic career."

"There are other things to do in the world," Lord Castleford said. "I have an Estate in England, a house where, when the War is over, I think you will be very happy, but in the meantime we shall be together. We can go to any neutral country we please and get to know each other. There is a lot I want to know about you, my beautiful one!"

"I cannot really believe you are saying such things to me," Yamina whispered. "It is so perfect, it is part of the sunshine, part of the music of the waves, but . . . I have to . . . persuade you that you are . . . making a terrible mistake!"

She moved from the shelter of his arms and said:

"Let me go away until the War is ended. We can write to each other, and then if our love withstands the test of time . . . that will be the moment to speak of marriage."

Lord Castleford laughed—it was the gay laugh of a man without care.

"My precious! Do you really think that I would let you out of my sight after what has happened already?" he enquired. "Look at the adventures in which you have been involved. Supposing the Turkish mob had found you and believed you to be a spy? Supposing you had not escaped from the Sultan's Harem? No! You need someone to look after you and that is what I intend to do."

"I will not marry you," Yamina said. "I will be your mistress. I will wait for you. I will do anything you like, but I will not be instrumental in depriving the diplomatic world of a man as important as you."

"No man is indispensable," Lord Castleford answered, "except to the woman who loves him. Could you find someone to replace me? Answer me that question."

Yamina gripped her fingers together.

"You know I could never find anyone to whom I could give my love, having once known you. You are right in saying this is different. This love we have for each other is . . . divine and has perhaps existed for thousands of years before we met again. But because it is so . . . special, it will not matter if we wait a . . . little."

"We are not going to wait!" Lord Castleford said firmly. "The Elchi believes that Sebastopol will fall in two or three months' time, which means there will be peace by Christmas—but I am not concerned. I want you, Yamina, now, and I intend to have you! Not as my mistress, my beautiful darling, but as my wife!"

"What can I say to you? How can I convince you you are making a mistake?" Yamina asked frantically.

He put his arms round her and turned her face up to his.

"This is the only argument to which I am prepared to listen!" he said and kissed her.

It seemed to Yamina that his kiss had something very spiritual and sacred in it, as if he dedicated himself to her.

Then as she thrilled to the touch of his lips and felt her body move against his she knew she had no more arguments, no more protests to make.

She loved him and their love carried them away into the sky where there were no problems, no difficulties, only a diffusion of light which came from the gods themselves.

A long time later, it might have been a century of passing time, Lord Castleford raised his head and looked down at Yamina's flushed and happy face.

There was a hint of fire in his eyes, there was also a tenderness in his expression that she had never seen before.

"Now tell me that anything is of importance except us and our love," he said softly.

"There is nothing," she answered, "you are the earth, the sky, the sea! You are my world . . . there is nothing in it but you!"

He made a little sound of triumph, then he was kissing her again with slow deliberate kisses which took her soul into his keeping. . . .

* * *

She argued with him again during the evening, but it was half-hearted.

Lord Castleford was calm and determined, with the air of a man who has made a monumental decision and no longer allows even the smallest detail of it to concern him.

He merely reiterated that when they arrived in Athens he would call on the King, as would be expected, then he would write immediately to London, sending his resignation to Lord Palmerston and saying merely that he would wait in Athens until another Minister could be sent to replace him.

"I owe the Foreign Office good manners, if nothing else," he said to Yamina, "but that need not deter us from making arrangements for our marriage to take place immediately."

"We belong to different . . . religions," she said faintly.

Lord Castleford shrugged his shoulders.

"We are both Christians, but it would not matter to me whether you were a Moslem or a Hotentot! All I am concerned with is that the Marriage-Service should be binding and that for you there is no escape."

"Do you imagine I should ever wish to leave you?" she asked in a low voice.

"I think I would kill you rather than lose you to another man!"

She gave a little laugh.

"If there are any other men in the world, I am unable to see them! You fill my eyes and you know as well as I do no man could be more handsome or attractive!"

"Are you flattering me?" Lord Castleford teased. "It is something you have never done before, Yamina!"

"There has never actually been an opportunity. Have you counted the hours we have known each other?"

"I knew you first in the Garden of Eden," Lord Castleford said, "and I met you again when I travelled across the world in the train of Marco Polo. Perhaps we were part of the hordes which rallied behind Genghis Khan, or maybe we lived in Crete in the golden age of King Minos."

Yamina clasped her hands together.

"How I wish Papa could hear you," she said. "Those are the civilisations which meant so much more to him than his own, and it was the history of those times that I used to read aloud to him."

Lord Castleford smiled.

"So we have something else in common, my precious."

When it grew late and it was time to go to bed Yamina looked at Lord Castleford and he saw the question in her eyes.

"I love you!" he said. "I also worship you for your purity and because you are enshrined in my heart."

He kissed the palms of both her hands, then he said:

"I want you! God knows, I want you! My body aches for you, but I will not make you mine until the ring is on your finger—until you are my wife, when no man, or creed, or Priest, or law may ever put us apart again."

Yamina put her arms round his neck and drew his head down to hers.

"I am ready to do . . . anything you . . . want of . . . me," she whispered.

"And that, my darling, is why I must protect you against myself," Lord Castleton said, "just as I will protect you for the rest of your life against anything which could harm or distress you. Against not only danger but also unhappiness, and, most of all, any regrets."

He kissed her until she was throbbing and pulsating with the fire he always awakened in her. Then he set her away from him, kissed her forehead, and said in a voice that was very deep:

"Go to bed, my beautiful darling. There is a great deal for us to do tomorrow."

He left her alone in the cabin.

Yamina heard him come back very much later.

She was awake but she did not speak to him, and after he had undressed Lord Castleford lay down on the cushions which Jenkins had prepared for him.

She knew from the way he turned and twisted from time to time that he was awake, as she was, but they did not speak to each other.

It was as if they had dedicated themselves to a certain course and an iron discipline prevented them from breaking it.

In the morning Lord Castleford rose early and went up on deck to see the ship steam into Piraeus, the Port of Athens.

Only when they were actually coming alongside the Quay did he return to the cabin to find that Yamina was ready to get into the painted trunk.

He looked at her for a moment in her crimson *entari* with the glittering girdle of precious stones and the brooch from her *talpock* pinning her chemise tightly at her neck, and he smiled.

"If they saw you walking in the streets of Athens you would cause a riot!" he said. "Cover yourself with your veil, my darling. There is a great deal to be said for the woman one loves being kept in purdah!"

Yamina laughed and lifted her face to his.

He held her very close and kissed her gently. Then as they heard the ship's engines slowing down and the cries and shouts of the sailors mooring her, Yamina stepped into the painted trunk, and Lord Castleford closed the lid and turned the key in the gold locks.

As he did so Jenkins came into the cabin.

"You have the rest of my luggage ready?" Lord Castleford asked.

"Yes, M'Lord!"

"Then go ashore as soon as we dock. Take a carriage to the British Residency, and as soon as you can get this trunk upstairs to my bed-room, let Miss Yamina out."

"I'll do that, M'Lord."

"I will follow as soon as possible," Lord Castleford said. "There will doubtless be a Reception-party from the Residency to meet me and I will also have to make my farewells to the Captain."

"I understand, M'Lord. I've already arranged for some stewards to help me ashore with our luggage."

"Then see they are very careful with this!"

"I will, M'Lord."

Yamina heard Lord Castleford go from the cabin. Then a short time later two stewards lifted her up and she felt herself being carried along the deck and down a gang-way onto the Quay.

Lord Castleford was right in thinking there would be a deputation to meet him.

All the Senior Officials of the Residential Staff came aboard to welcome him to Athens.

His reputation had gone before him, and he knew they were delighted and impressed that anyone so well-known should be appointed as Minister Plenipotentiary in Greece, which was a trouble-spot.

There was a great deal they wanted to tell him and he was further delayed when he found that the Captain wished him and the members of his staff to join him in his cabin. There was wine and food and a wearisome exchange of toasts before he could go ashore.

Afterwards there were various Officials in charge of the wounded soldiers who wanted to offer him their good wishes on his new appointment, and it was in fact afternoon before Lord Castleford found himself driving through the colourful streets of Athens.

King Otho had made Athens the Capital of Greece partly in deference to the classical interests of his father, King Ludovic I of Bavaria.

Under the Turks, Athens had degenerated into little more than a fishing village, and it had grown up overnight into a conglomeration of booths and Palaces.

Great numbers of the population lived and slept in the streets, as there was an acute shortage of houses, but Athens had a picturesque charm which was, Lord Castleford thought, more Oriental than Western.

The noisy streets were crowded with exotic costumes.

There were rich Moldavian nobles riding fine horses who looked out of place beside the austerity of the Monks moving up and down the steps of the dark iron-studded Churches.

There were Albanians to whom the Capital was the zenith of amusement, wearing crimson and gold embroideries, bristling with pistols, their horses trapped out in gold and silver.

It was all a mixture of Slav, Turk, and Levantine, Bavarian introduced by the King, and the classical Greek of bygone years.

It constituted, Lord Castleford knew, a challenge that he would have enjoyed and looked forward to, if he had not already decided it was no longer any of his business and that he would be leaving Greece in a very short time.

The British Residency was impressive and very different from most of the other Ministries and Consulates which, owing to lack of accommodation, were situated in narrow, dirty streets or even lodged in Inns.

It was reassuring to see the Union Jack blowing in the breeze, the garden laid out with neat and tidy flower-beds, the servants wearing quietly impressive livery, and to feel the conventional black-and-white marble floor of the Hall under his feet.

There were still formalities that had to be observed, secretaries, clerks, and senior-servants to be presented, and although Lord Castleford was impatient he was too well trained to appear anything but courteous and grateful for the attention that was being paid to him.

It seemed to him, however, that a century of time had passed since he had last seen Yamina, as he hurried up the stairs to his private Suite of rooms on the first floor overlooking the garden.

Jenkins was waiting for him on the landing, and as he saw Lord Castleford approach he opened the door and he walked into the Sitting-Room.

There was no sign of the painted trunk, and he was gazing across the large room to the door which he knew must lead into the bed-room when Jenkins said in a low voice:

"Miss Yamina has gone, M'Lord!"

"What do you mean—gone?" Lord Castleford asked sharply.

"I had the painted trunk carried upstairs first as soon as we arrived at the Residency," Jenkins replied. "I impressed on the servants to be extremely careful with it, M'Lord."

"Yes, yes!" Lord Castleford said. "What happened?"

"I ordered the rest of the luggage to follow, M'Lord, then went ahead to let out Miss Yamina, as you told me to do."

"She was all right?" Lord Castleford enquired.

"Perfectly, M'Lord! She thanked me for having taken so much care in bringing her from the ship."

"Then what happened?"

"I went out of the bed-room, M'Lord, and directed the disposal of your luggage in a wardrobe-room which is part of your Suite. It took me some time and, because I thought Miss Yamina would wish to be alone, I started to unpack the clothes I thought Your Lordship would require so that they would not become too creased by remaining in the trunks."

"I understand," Lord Castleford said impatiently.

He always found Jenkins's long-winded narratives irritating.

"Then, after a little time, M'Lord, I went to find out if there was anything Miss Yamina would require, but she was no longer there!"

"She was no longer there?"

Lord Castleford's voice was harsh.

"She'd gone, M'Lord!"

"How could she have done? Someone must have seen her."

Jenkins hesitated a moment.

"I noticed, M'Lord," he said after a moment, "that before we left the ship a sheet was missing from the bed on which Miss Yamina had slept. I thought she must have put it in the trunk to make it more comfortable, but there is no sign of it here and she must have worn it in order to leave the Residency."

"Worn it?" Lord Castleford ejaculated.

Even as he spoke he knew that that was the answer.

There was no difference between a white sheet and a *ferejeh*, which every Oriental woman wore.

In the streets, in the Turkish Bazaar of the Capital, there would be innumerable women wearing *ferejehs*, the garments covering them completely so that there was nothing distinctive about their features except for their eyes.

He realised that because of the excitement of his arrival in the Residency it would have been easy for Yamina to slip down a back staircase, find a side-door, and disappear.

That she had done so struck him like a blow.

He could not believe that she would leave him,

could not credit after all they had said to each other, after all they had planned, that she would walk out of his life as mysteriously as she had come into it.

Too late, he thought that perhaps in her own way she was as determined as he was.

She had cried out against his sacrificing his career on her behalf, and while he had the feeling they would never lose each other completely, he thought that perhaps she was putting her own plan into operation.

That was to stay away from him until the War was over and they need no longer, as representatives of their different countries, be officially enemies.

"She cannot mean it! She cannot intend to do that!" Lord Castleford told himself, and yet he was afraid.

Now he cursed himself for not having forced Yamina to tell him more about herself.

It seemed incredible, unbelievable, but he still did not know her name.

As she had said, it seemed so unimportant and one Russian name was very like another.

'My darling! My precious!' he cried out to her in his heart. 'How can you do this to me? How can you make me suffer so intolerably?'

Only the self-control he had exercised all his life prevented him from crying out loud at his suffering.

He knew Jenkins was watching him apprehensively in case he should be blamed for what had happened, and automatically he said:

"It was not your fault, Jenkins. Make enquiries—very discreetly, of course—in case anybody noticed Miss Yamina leaving the Residency and learned where she was going."

"I'll do that, M'Lord," Jenkins said with an expression of relief on his face.

Lord Castleford walked to the window to stare out with unseeing eyes at the hills and mountains that encircled Athens.

They were very beautiful in the sunshine but he saw only two dark eyes looking into his, and felt a soft mouth that quivered when he touched it.

"I will find her again," he told himself, "even if it takes me a life-time to do so!"

Deep in his thoughts, Jenkins's voice seemed to come from a long way away as the Valet said:

"Excuse me, M'Lord, but it's time you were changing for your visit to the Palace."

Lord Castleford took a deep breath, his sense of duty took control, and for the time being the bitter chaos of his feelings gave way to the discipline of years.

Automatically, hardly aware what he was doing, he allowed Jenkins to assist him into the diplomatic uniform that he must wear when he presented his credentials to the King of the Hellenes.

The silk stockings, the black knee-breeches, and the coat copiously embroidered with gold thread were the trappings which in the past had filled him with pride.

Now he was like a doll in Jenkins's hands, and when finally he was dressed he did not even pause to glance at himself in the mirror.

He went down the broad staircase, and his gloves and triangular hat were waiting for him in the Hall.

There was a closed carriage outside and the sentries came smartly to attention as he stepped into it.

The two horses drew him down the narrow drive and into the street seething with people.

Lord Castleford leant forward.

Perhaps among them, he thought, he would catch sight of Yamina.

But he knew he would be unable to recognise her. There were so many women wearing *ferejehs,* some white, some black, the Moslems in the dull indecisive grey which made them look like shadows.

They reached the Palace.

The soldiers were splendid in the *fustanella*—stiff, pleated white skirts which were worn with heavily encrusted gold boleros, tasselled caps set rakishly to one side of their dark heads, and cummerbunds holding daggers.

The huge square building had been started by King Otho when he first came to the throne, but he became bored with it and it was finally his father, King Ludwig, who finished it.

The great high Salons glittered with crystal chandeliers. The baroque carving, the gilded furniture, and the wealth of porcelain was all in the Bavarian tradition.

Lord Castleford was expected and was led by a resplendent Major-Domo across the Hall to where two flunkeys flung open two magnificently painted doors.

An Aide-de-Camp with liquid black eyes, which wrought havoc amongst the impressionable women of other nations, greeted Lord Castleford and led him through to another door flanked by footmen.

It was opened and Lord Castleford saw King Otho and Queen Amelie waiting for him at the far end.

He advanced and as he bowed the Aide-de-Camp announced:

"His Excellency, Lord Castleford, Minister Plenipotentiary for Great Britain, Your Majesty!"

King Otho had thickened since he came to the throne, but he still had the Bavarian good looks which had swept so many beautiful women unprotestingly into his arms.

"Welcome to Greece!" he said in English.

Lord Castleford bent over his hand with the conventional:

"You are very gracious, Sire."

The Queen held out her hand.

She had aged more obviously than her husband, but she was still, Lord Castleford noted, undoubtedly an attractive woman.

"We have been looking forward to your arrival, My Lord," she said. "It is a long time since last we saw you."

"It is indeed, Ma'am!" Lord Castleford agreed.

"We have a guest staying with us," the Queen said, "who is very anxious to make your acquaintance."

As she spoke she glanced towards a door which stood behind them and as if at an arranged signal a woman came into the Salon.

Lord Castleford glanced at her indifferently, then suddenly he was still.

It was Yamina advancing towards him, a very different Yamina from the one he had last seen slipping into the painted trunk in the cabin of the *Himalaya.*

She was wearing a large crinoline draped with pink chiffon, caught with little bunches of water-lilies.

Her bodice, which revealed the curves of her exquisite figure, was buttoned to the neck. Her waist was very small and her hair was arranged in fashionable ringlets on either side of her face.

She looked exquisitely lovely, and yet as her eyes met Lord Castleford's he thought there was an expression of apprehension in them, as if she was afraid he would be angry with her.

"I wish to present, My Lord," the Queen said, "Her Serene Highness, Princess Yamina Yurievski. I think you met her late father, the Grand Duke Ivan, when you were in Russia."

It was impossible for Lord Castleford to move or speak. He could only look at Yamina, and as if she understood what he was feeling she turned her head with an expression of pleading on her face towards the King.

He smiled as he said to Lord Castleford:

"Yamina, whom I have known since she was a child, has brought me a difficult problem, My Lord. She says she wishes to marry you immediately! She also tells me that you feel in the circumstances that you must resign from your position as British Minister."

"That is my intention, Sire," Lord Castleford replied.

"I think that would be a great loss to Greece, if we should lose you at this difficult moment in our history."

"You are very flattering, Sire," Lord Castleford replied, "but Your Majesty is well aware that as we are at war with Russia it would be impossible for the British Minister to have a Russian wife."

"That is the problem with which Yamina has presented me," King Otho said. "But because I really consider myself extremely clever, I have a solution!"

Lord Castleford did not speak.

But Yamina knew by the expression on his face that he had no hope that any solution the King might suggest would be acceptable to the Foreign Office in London.

"I do not think you know," the King went on, "or you may have forgotten, that the Grand Duke Ivan married Princess Athene of Peloponnese."

Lord Castleford looked surprised.

"It was a marriage that was frowned upon at the time by the Tsar, and Princess Athene when she left Greece made over her Estates to her nephew, the only surviving member of that ancient Greek family."

Yamina was watching Lord Castleford's face and he was listening attentively to the King.

"The Prince, as it happens, was killed two years ago in a revolution," His Majesty continued, "and because he was fighting against the Crown his lands were confiscated."

He turned his head to smile at Yamina.

"Because I think it right, now that Yamina has come to me and asked for my help and protection, I intend to transfer to her what were her grand-father's lands in Peloponnese. But there is a condition attached to the gift."

"A condition, Sire?" Lord Castleford asked, because he felt that the King was waiting for him to speak.

"Yes, a condition," King Otho said. "It is that Yamina should take Greek nationality. She will no longer be Her Serene Highness, but Princess Yamina of Peloponnese."

He saw the sudden light that came into Lord Castleford's eyes and added with a smile:

"I cannot imagine that Lord Palmerston, or any member of the Foreign Office in London, would object to their Minister at this moment making sure of Greece's neutrality by taking a Greek wife."

Yamina made a little sound of happiness and as if she could contain herself no longer she slipped her hand into Lord Castleford's.

His fingers closed over hers so tightly that it was painful.

Then he said in a voice that he controlled with difficulty:

"How can I thank Your Majesty?"

"By staying to dinner and telling me of your adventures both in Persia and in Constantinople," the King replied. "I feel I must catch up with world events outside my own turbulent country."

"I shall be delighted to accept your invitation, Sire," Lord Castleford said.

He bowed and Yamina ran to the King to lift her face to his.

"Thank you! Thank you!" she said. "I cannot tell you how happy you have made us!"

King Otho touched her cheek as he said:

"You are nearly as beautiful as your mother, my dear."

Then as Yamina sank down in a deep curtsey the King and Queen withdrew through the door by which Yamina had entered the Salon and were followed by the Aide-de-Camp.

Lord Castleford waited until the door had closed behind them, then put his arms round Yamina.

"My wonderful, incredible, darling!" he cried. "How did you manage it, and why did you not tell me?"

"I was not sure the King would receive me," Yamina replied. "It is twenty years since Mama ran away from Greece to marry Papa. I thought perhaps King Otho would still be annoyed that she had never returned."

"He has been very kind," Lord Castleford said automatically, but his eyes were on Yamina's face.

"I think the truth is that he had a certain tenderness for Mama," Yamina smiled. "She was very beautiful!"

"And so are you, my darling," Lord Castleford said, "more beautiful than I can ever tell you. How soon can we be married?"

"As soon as I am a Greek citizen," Yamina replied, "which will be tomorrow!"

"I cannot wait—you know that!"

"I will help you in all you have to do here," Yamina said softly, "that is . . . if you will let me."

"All I want is for you to be with me and never to leave me," Lord Castleford said. "I am not certain now that I am really pleased that I still have to go on with my career. I should be completely and utterly happy to have nothing to do but make love to you!"

"I would always have been afraid that one day you might come to the conclusion that the sacrifice was not worthwhile," Yamina said simply.

"Do you really believe I could ever think that?"

He drew her into his arms and his voice deepened as he said:

"I love you! It will take a whole life-time to tell you how much! As you have said yourself, there is nothing in the world except our love!"

He looked down at the happiness in her eyes and said with a little smile:

"So the slave-girl was really a Princess in disguise! It is the right ending to a fairy-story!"

"No . . . she will always be a . . . slave," Yamina whispered, "your slave, now and forever!"

"We are both the slaves of love," Lord Castleford said. "A love, my darling, which has existed since the beginning of time and will exist until Heaven and earth shall pass away!"

As he spoke his lips sought hers and as Yamina felt his mouth take possession of her she felt once again the flame within her come alive.

She knew that it echoed the fire of Lord Castleford's lips and the fire in his eyes which told her how much he desired her.

It was love—violent, tempestuous, overwhelming, as invincible, as he had said himself, as the burning heat of the sun, and there was no escape.

They were the slaves of its Majesty, now and forever!

ABOUT THE AUTHOR

BARBARA CARTLAND, the celebrated romantic author, historian, playwright, lecturer, political speaker and television personality, has now written over 150 books. Miss Cartland has had a number of historical books published and several biographical ones, including that of her brother, Major Ronald Cartland, who was the first Member of Parliament to be killed in the War. This book had a Foreword by Sir Winston Churchill.

In private life, Barbara Cartland, who is a Dame of the Order of St. John of Jerusalem, has fought for better conditions and salaries for Midwives and nurses. As President of the Royal College of Midwives (Hertfordshire Branch), she has been invested with the first Badge of Office ever given in Great Britain, which was subscribed to by the Midwives themselves. She has also championed the cause of old people and founded the first Romany Gypsy Camp in the world.

Barbara Cartland is deeply interested in Vitamin Therapy and is President of the British National Association for Health.